White Knees of Hanoi Series

White Knees of Hanoi Series

BISHOP'S PACKAGE

A.M. Hamilton

To order additional copies of this book, contact:
Xlibris Corporation
1-888-795-4274
www.Xlibris.com
Orders@Xlibris.com
112549

CHAPTER 1

A medic with the 101st Airborne Division once told Bishop, "this ain't gona hurt much," but the pain that followed the tetracycline shot for clap made it very difficult to sit down for several days. Now, standing across the boulevard from Company Headquarters of the Royal Canadian Army Engineer Battalion, Bishop pondered the significance of that particular phrase again.

But the disciplinary action Bishop was being summoned for was of a different sort. It was a matter of honor that compelled the twenty four year old Corporal to revolt against another trooper when it was made very public that Bishop was a turn coat Yankee. In fact it was just the opposite. Bishop had been born and raised in Canada and only went to the States when he couldn't join the Canadian forces due to age requirements. Ironically, when he served in the American forces he was constantly teased for joining the service when most American's were running to Canada to avoid the draft.

When Bishop joined the American army he was full of spunk and prurience. It was the result of an unhappy childhood, a lack of contentment, and a learned sense of selective loyalty. Throughout his childhood he always felt different from the rest. There was a nagging sense of being older, even in cases when he was. Not just in age, but in advancement. A curious word that in a roundabout way defined for him a course of life that brought him to this very spot at this appropriate time. His high school teacher might have agreed with Karl Jong's theory of synchronicity. One event following another that leads to a more prominent conclusion.

For the most part Bishop was an arrow of a man with a stride that was bubbling with confidence. His green eyes clicked with interest in those things of interest and spoke of too many late night endeavors.

The November winds were up to their usual stuff as Bishop crossed the double wide road to reach the median at Trenton Air Force Base. Combined forces bases were still years off but in some parts of the military system small nudges to consolidate helped with defense budgets.

Reaching the opposite side of the road he walked past the sign that once proclaimed B Company Headquarters had now been changed to Mobil Force Management and Logistics. The moniker had a more professional ring to it, but did little to instill confidence in the abilities of those who served.

The one thing that remained the same, but only temporarily, was the three story building that was still painted sky blue, the color of its previous owners, the air force.

Bishops footsteps plundered along the narrow concrete hallways as he made for Major Clifford's office on the second floor. Poorly lit, the polished wooden plaques along-side of each oak doorway was difficult to read, but it didn't matter Bishop knew precisely where to go. He wasn't a regular visitor, yet.

Bishop had noticed that when you're in trouble, you were never bothered with the usual affable greeting by the office secretary. Instead a silent blur as the door was opened into Clifford's office was all you could expect.

With as much pomp as he could muster Bishop swaggered in and snapped to attention directly in front of a smiling hulk that possessed the bearing of a small bear cub lost in the woods.

"Corporal Bishop reporting sir!"

The door politely clicked shut behind as Bishops eyes quickly scanned the empty desk top before him. The only item was a closed record file folder with Canadian Forces Recruit stamped in red on the cover. There were a few scribbled signatures indicating it had been sent around.

"I have some news for you Corporal; you won't be put up on charge for your little prank yesterday. Sargent Lead is claiming he slipped on the wet floor, again."

"Oh yes sir, I'm sure that's what happened sir."

"Sit down," the Major said in a managerial tone.

"Thank you sir."

"Now," Clifford said opening the file in front of him. "Looking through your record I see you joined the US Army in the summer of 1968 at the age of seventeen."

"Seventeen and a half sir. I needed a note from my mom to get in."

"And that was after we booted you out for lying about your age?"

"Yes sir."

"So why the American Army?"

"I was running away from home and I needed a job."

"And you obviously found one."

"Yes sir."

"According to you record I see that you were awarded a substantial list of military honors while in Vietnam. In fact, you're probably one of the most decorated soldiers we have if you base it on foreign awards," Clifford commented firmly.

Bishop mustered a friendly nod.

"How do you like being in the Canadian Forces?"

"I feel I have retired sir."

"Retired?" Clifford said somewhat puzzled.

"Yes sir, I went form a fighting army to one on vacation."

"I see," Clifford felt he had run into the kind of response he got from deserters. But Bishop wasn't one of those. He was fighter that needs a great deal of guidance if he were to remain in service.

"The Army is my life sir. I'm not married and I don't have any kids I know of. So this is where I belong."

"Yes, well I think there's going to be a change in your life."

"Sir?"

"I have a set of orders for you, they came down yesterday actually. Due to your past experience you're being sent to Hanoi Vietnam as a peacekeeper," Clifford said with a wry grin.

There was a pause coming from the Corporal that seemed to last an hour. He hadn't joined the service to see the same part of the world the American's had already showed him.

"Sir," Bishop began as he sat up in his chair. "You've got to believe me I'm all for a little peace, but when the other guy is trying to kill you it make's things very difficult."

"Well that was because you were with the Americans who are war with the North. We are a peacekeeping force recording violations on the belligerent parties for United Nations regulators."

"Yea but sir."

Holding up his hand Major Clifford said, "Orders are orders Corporal, you know that. And I would suggest you be a little less Americanized when you're over there."

"Americanized?"

"A broader use of the word eh, and less swearing."

Bishop slumped back min his chair, "Well sir, I guess I can bloody well do that eh!"

Clifford smirked, "Well it's a start."

CHAPTER 2

When all the formalities of reassignment had been completed Bishop found himself partway through the cold month of January. But this New Year and new posting made the cold feel warmer. Not so much on the skin but internally.

For most of his leave time Bishop amused himself with reading hastened articles of Vietnam in the mid-section of the Toronto Sun. He was amazed by how little of it was original to Canadian press sources. There seemed to be a constant drum beat focused on another Canadian trying to induct Boston into the Stanly Cup playoffs for the third year running.

Several articles appeared mentioning that the North Vietnamese had shuttled in and out of the peace talks in Paris, and that TET 72 would be lack luster in their quest to concur the South. Bishop was grateful for Nixon's attempts knowing that lunch is a lot more digestible when you're not being shot at.

Occasionally a stray thought ricocheted around in Bishops mind like a confused bullet trying to find its way out of an armored vehicle. 'If I'm not a combatant, but a peacekeeper, does that make me a spy?'

This query was very perplexing. A spy, Bishop thought had to be smart, resourceful, cunning all knowing, and sexy. At least according to Ion Fleming. In short, an over achiever with a bent toward self-indulgence.

But Bishop was none of these. In fact he was nearly the exact opposite. Yes, he had proven himself in combat, but his romantic side tended to keep him on sick call a lot. "It must be love," he kept telling the medics.

When Prime Minister Trudeau went to China for trade negotiations, Air Canada was already there with five flights a week to Hong Kong. It was the heart pounding transit flight from Hong Kong to Hanoi International airport on a twin engine turbo prop that proved to be a handful. For some strange reason every time the plane made a turn either way, the engines slowed and sputtered until resurrected by level flight. More disconcerting was the fact that the other passengers, mostly oriental types with two Russians, seemed least affected.

In the gradual decent into Hanoi's archaic passenger facility the plane banked to the right and out Bishops side window he could see the long dwindling line of the Red River as it made its way toward the Laotian boarder, and the old battlement of DienBienPhue. Another turn displayed a slip of black smoke in the distant locale of Haiphong Harbor. Courtesy of the US Navy he deduced.

Directly below him Bishop could see the encroaching landscape pot marked by patterned bombing runs from Air Force jets. On closer inspection he could see the circular grave sites of former living families that seemed to fade into the pre-monsoon sky. The rice patties where merely boxes of water integrated into drab green jungle. At this altitude, people were undistinguishable.

Another shudder and then a whining sound took Bishop's attention from the ground to his current position. It was then he noticed the landing flaps had been extended and guessed the shutter had to be attributed to that pot holed section of the highway in the sky.

It was then he spotted the hostess, or what was a reasonable imitation of the female gender in a French sundress teetering toward him. Her presence was noticed several times over the course of the trip as she made numerous ports of call on the two Russians that seemed eager for another vodka chaser.

Bishop extended his hand as if he was waving down an oncoming taxi driven by a half in the bag operator. "When are we landing!"

The noise in the cabin muffled his voice but she understood and shuffled toward him.

"We pancake in fen minuets sir!" she replied steading herself against the back of the empty seat in front of him. "You tie up now,"

"Say what?"

"You tie up now," she reiterated then reaching down motioned for Bishop to fasten his seat belt.

"Oh yea, right." He replied.

"You Canada?"

"Yes, how could you guess?"

"You sound like American GI." She replied and then turned her attention to her Soviet guest's two rows up.

"Yea right," then added, "eh!"

Hanoi International Airport was actually a contradiction in terms. In its humble beginnings it was nothing more than a dirt strip for passenger flights from Saigon to Canton China. Merely a refueling stop as passengers enjoyed tea and cakes while maintenance was being performed. Then after the Second World War the French added a couple of new runways to accommodate larger passenger planes. Due to the encirclement of the peasant population there was no room to add again when jet airliners prowled the skies.

As for the international part, the small airdrome could only manage STOL (Short Take Off and Landing), type planes which is what Bishop was riding in. Typically not known for lavish accommodations, these aircraft are more associated with hard landings and breakfast losing take offs.

The exhausted craft took a nose dive attitude and Bishop clutched the armrests with a death grip typical of women who grab their gynecologists' arm when informed she had just become pregnant by the wrong man.

With terra firma less than a hundred feet below the slums of Hanoi became blatantly obvious. Tin roofs covered over once splendid French villas and the park where long ago French tourists strolled to enjoy the cool summer breezes sent down from the highlands to the west was now nothing more than a bombed out parking lot. The streets were jammed with bicycles and cycle taxi's surrounded by a sea of round bamboo bonnets.

With his ears popping in response to the sudden drop in air pressure Bishop watched from his window as the former rice paddies switched to tire marked concrete and the bang as the plane landed. Engines sputtering and G force yanking at his winter dress green uniform he pushed himself hard back into his seat until the forward movement became more tolerable.

The craft limped into what was once a modern terminal now riddled with bullet holes and rocket impact craters to finally succumb in front of the only working door to the building. A couple of men dressed in Chinese Army flight suites walked slowly toward the craft dragging a small step ladder.

When the cabin door opened the escaping pressurized air made it sounded more like a sigh of relief then a welcome to sea level. With the real monsoon a few months off, the tears of China is what the locals called it, plundered the field leaving hundreds of bird baths in the uneven pavement. This steady weather pattern was typical for the first few months of the new-year. In fact it made the TET celebrations rather dreary in the north, so much so the typical launching of fireworks was nearly always rained out.

Bishop was first off being seated near the rear door, followed by a handful of Vietnamese men and the two Russians who navigated with a wonky compass.

Once inside the terminal, lit only by flickering neon lights suspended from the cracked plaster ceiling, Bishop, being the only member dressed in official looking attire, was ushered by two guards in black pajama like uniforms to a counter.

"Pissport," the North Vietnamese officer demanded.

Bishop reached for the inside pocket of his tunic when a resilient hand snatched his wrist and held tightly. A jabbing in the lower back reminded Bishop of a PPK nine millimeter pistol.

"What the ffff, EH!" Bishop yelled.

"YOU STOP!" called the officer excitedly.

Bishop paused as the officer rounded the counter and stuck his hand inside Bishops dress coat. With a pinch to his chest Bishop's passport was extracted and thumbed through.

"You Canook, first time Vietnam?"

"That's right," Bishop replied with a less aggressive attitude.

He was in one of those situations that usually ended badly. Even learning his lesson he knew that one wrong twitch could end with a rifle butt stroke to the head. It was then he glanced about the darkened room to find he was alone, except for the duty people. The other passengers had already left the building.

The officer was oddly the same height as Bishop but possessed a natural dislike for round eyes, particularly ones that spoke English. He had served with the Viet Cong Army prior to its demise and was relocated to Hanoi after TET 1968. Far from his family he grew more disgusted with the lengthening of the war, even though the propaganda ministry was claiming huge victories in the South. Those who knew, were less understanding of the feint.

"Where bag?"

"What?"

"Where BAG! You got bag?"

Bishop understood the bad English and pointed in the direction of the plane.

"You go get, me see," the officer demanded and handed the passport back to Bishop.

"You got to be shitten me Ralph?" Bishop muttered as he turned toward the door.

"WHAT, What you say GI?"

Bishop paused then turned back to the officer. "Merry Christmas, eh" Bishop replied.

The Officer glared then waved him on.

It was then a door in the far corner opened and the brightness of the overcast day filled the void as a blackened silhouette strolled in with all the demeanor of a dash hound.

"Corporal Bishop!" the shape hollered.

"SIR!" Bishop responded and snapped to attention. Frozen in place he wondered why the cavalry wore shorts with boney white knees.

"This man is under diplomatic protection Lieutenant Ho Buc. How many times must I tell you?" Captain La Roach exclaimed in a firm tone as if scolding a young child.

Ho Buc stood taught like a knife ready to plunge, giving no ground. He hated being told what to do by foreigners, even invited ones.

"Go get your kit Bishop and double around the building to street side."

"Yes sir," Bishop replied and trotted off like a dear just missing a broadside by an eighteen wheeler.

CHAPTER 3

The Ministry of Defense was continually underfunded and as a result all the good stuff was kept near Ottawa for holiday parades. For the overseas NATO Defense Forces they had to scrounge up what they needed and usually bought their vehicles locally. But the trucks the North was selling were cast offs of Soviet Iveco's who's prime was spent chasing German's from Stalingrad.

It was only by sheer coincidence that the 1968 Ford pickup painted Pepsi blue arrived in Hanoi as part of an agricultural exchange. It wasn't clear as to what the North exchanged it for, but the truck looked as though it had spent most of its life dodging hail storms in Kansas.

With the large white letters UNNV painted on the door and the Canadian flag painted on the hood it was apparent to anyone who saw it, the truck wasn't from around here. Even more insulting, the other two UN observers were Warsaw Pact armies. Their vehicles were usually Mercedes and painted annually to keep up appearances.

The first thing a soldier learns, and this is true in all occasions, never leave anything of value in the back. As a result Captain La Roach, Corporal Bishop and Private First Collins, who went by his Christian name John, were crammed into the cab with Bishops duffle bag between his legs. With the defroster not working and Bishop in his winter dress uniform most of the ride was spent clearing the windows of humidity.

The struggle for foot space was constant as each man tried to find some relief from the unevenness of the sand bags covering the floor. A nuisance worth tolerating as it was the only protection from land minds.

Bishop glanced at the Captain and made an instant appraisal of his qualities, a habit combatants acquire as a result of necessity. One has to know if a man can be trusted in times of emergency.

La Rouch was like a pissed off giraffe. His temperament seemed to be chaffing the seams of his character. With close set dark eyes La Rouch looked like a man who had long conversations with water buffaloes.

As the truck glided its way down To Yong Street surrounded by a sea of cyclists it felt like being a turtle clinging to a log trapped in a muddy current.

"You have your travel papers Mr. Bishop?" La Rouch asked casually.

"Yes sir, in my bag."

"Your assignment here only includes three jobs," La Rouch began. "First you will be in charge of making sure our beacon is on every night. That's more important than your life."

"You can say that again boss," John piped in.

"Beacon sir?" Bishop asked.

"Yes, we have a radio transmission dish on the roof. You take the cover off at nine o'clock and then switch it on. At two PM you'll switch off and put the cover back on."

"What signal are you transmitting sir?"

"Well, all you need to know is that it's our CBC news being sent out. It took months for our cultural ministry to get permission from the North to do it, and we have to send out every night at the same time regardless."

Bishop was puzzled and wondered who in the North would be listening to Canadian News, especially when the North was sure to have its own propaganda stations going full tilt.

"Your second duty is to make three runs a week to the airport, pick up our supplies and any mail for the embassy. Sergeant Wilkins will take you through it the first time," La Rouch added." The last job will be on call for investigations and being my driver."

"What investigations?" Bishop asked

"We are here to investigate any infractions of the cease fire agreement by any of the belligerent parties. It especially applies to your American friends."

"Sir, I'm not an American."

"You aren't Canadian either pal," John said wryly.

"What is it with you guys?"

"Loyalties can be misplaced and why they sent you here is beyond me," La Rouch said.

"Okay, okay, let's get this shit straight. I was born and raised in Canada and just because you wouldn't take me on I went to the State's and they did. Is that a crime or what?"

"We are a professional Army Mr. Bishop and that means we serve only one master. Is that clear?"

"Clear as mud SIR!"

La Rouch wiped the moisture form his side window with the back of his hand. "Okay John make your turn."

John glanced through the back window, also foggy and turned sharply. The horde of cyclists that mingled with them since the airport parted like the Red Sea as the truck made a turn onto a less busy side street.

"They're out in force today aren't they?" Bishop commented.

"They are out in force EH" John said. It was an attempt to mock Bishop and was becoming more of a game then an attempt to make him sound more Canadian.

"It's market day. It'll be like this usually." John said.

"It'll be like this usually EH!" Bishop responded quickly.

There was a pause as the truck rolled past a bombed out building. Then looking over at the others John said, "I think he's getting it sir."

"Let's hope so. Our hosts are always watching us."

*   *   *

Group 6, United Nations North Vietnam was nicely painted on the plaster wall surrounding the compound. The three foot letters in white were painted over a light blue square. The announcement appeared to the masses as being one of at least five other groups when in fact it was one of only two other groups. Group 5 was just outside Haiphong Harbor on the coast, the other was group 2 just north of the Demilitarized Zone. In a small hamlet called Lung Me Trout, Group 2 was to oversee any invasions by the South which had as much chance of succeeding as an inebriated driver convincing a patrol man that he only had just one.

Beyond the collapsed gate of the compound were three main buildings. Once a French chateau owned by a mercantile salesman Group 6 had the derisory duty of trying to resurrect a once ostentatious symbol of decadence into a defendable outpost of fairness.

The main building, the chateau itself was divided into living quarters were each member had his own room on the second floor while offices, mess hall, and supply occupied the first floor. A small three stall garage was directly across the drive in front of the chateau while a machine shed formed the back corner of the seven foot high bastion wall. The shed is what the privates had turned into their own enlisted man's club.

Bishop climbed from the vehicle dragging his duffle bag behind him. Glancing around he spotted a small vegetable garden between the garage and the shed. It was neatly sectioned off with rows of various vegetables holding their own plot. Beyond the surrounding walls were roof tops of tin and leafless trees looking as if they were trying to spy on the Canadians.

"Nice little food supply," Bishop said as John walked around the front of the truck to join him.

Turning John's eyes scanned the top of the wall, "Yea, if we can keep the damn kids from stealing our stuff."

"We had the same problem down South," Bishop replied. "I could rig a frag to one of those cabbages if you want."

"Sorry Yank, we don't have any hand grenades and it would really piss off the boss if we did that."

Bishop simply smiled because he was kidding and he knew his tone was misunderstood by John. To him, John was a broad shouldered man whose attitude seemed to say, 'okay I'm here, now what?' Life was taken as it came, not by design, but by lack of interest. The gaze of John's blue eyes seemed to be dedicated to the contemplation of all the variables.

La Rouch was near the front veranda when he called back to the others. "Okay Corporal, John will show you your room and we eat at six. That should give you time to get acquainted with the rest of the group," La Rouch said.

"Yes sir!" Bishop replied with a snappy salute.

"Ah, we don't do that here Corporal. Not much point eh!" John said with a grin.

"I guess," Bishop replied and was ushered to his room on the second floor.

CHAPTER 4

It felt strange, Bishop thought, to sit down to a single table with linen, china, and a complete silverware set. It was like having an epiphany, but if you were an agnostic it was more of a warning that something very bad was headed your way.

The mess or dining room had ten foot ceilings and a propane gas camping lamp was hanging where the chandelier used to be. Large floor to ceiling windows opened to the veranda near the entrance and provided a splendid view of the garage. The attached smoking room which was through two large doors had been converted to a game room of sorts. Anyone was welcome but traditionally Sergeant Wilkins presided over festivities.

That was why the Privates had made their own club in the garden shed. They thought they would have more privacy in their deliberations.

Bishop was seated next to Bill, who was a Private Second Class, which only meant he had been in the army the required amount of time for the next promotion.

Bill was a slightish man and standing in formation one could hear the wind whistling about his knees. Sober of thought and religious of routine, Bill was the perfect lackey always expecting his promotion.

Across from Bishop was Ed also a Private Second. Curiously Ed was a college graduate whose obscure degree was free formed to match course credit requisites. In certain circles he would be called a fresh air graduate, his degree being in Lunar History. If they ever decided to grow goldfish on Mars, Ed would be perfect for the directorship.

Captain La Rouch was at one end of the table while Sergeant Wilkins ruminated at the other. John also served as the unit cook and a Private First Class, which meant he was at the bottom of the totem. In all, the group, as Bishop saw them, were somewhat of a band of inimical brothers. A common occurrence when people are confined in a small space.

"So, when do we eat?" Bill queried with folded hands hovering over his plate.

Ed leaned back in his seat and peered through the doorway across the formal reception area at the entry to the kitchen. "He's coming," was Ed's response.

"Corporal," La Rouch asked. "Were you issued summer dress before coming over?"

Bishop, still clad in his winter uniform replied, "No sir."

"Then Sergeant Wilkins will see to it that you have proper dress at tomorrow's formation."

Sergeant Wilkins looked up from staring at his empty plate. "Sir, where will I get Mr. Bishop's summers dress?"

"From supply of course. We're equipped for thirty members."

"Sir, we're equipped for thirty troopers who are already dressed for the season."

"Well order some up from Ottawa!'

"Sir, that request will take months."

It was at this juncture John slipped in loaded with a tray full ration tins. Quietly he went to each place and sat one of the metal containers on the plate of each disappointed consumer.

"Then talk to your Polish friends, their uniforms are close to ours."

"Their shorts are darker than ours."

"Then wash them until they match. Good God do I have to think of everything." La Rouch declared as he snapped his napkin and drew it across his lap.

"Sir!" Wilkins retorted with disdain. He didn't like being run down by the officer in front of the other men. Especially the new man, Bishop.

"Was there a game this morning?" Ed asked as he scooped his ration from the tin onto his plate.

Bill pulled what looked like a book mark from his top pocket and scanned the row of information. "Yep, Leaf's and Wing's at Detroit."

Someone cried, "Go LEAF's"

"Not a chance eh?" Bill replied with a sneer. The corner of the listing caught on the edge of his pocket and he had to jiggle it to go in.

"Do up your button Bill."

"Right Sergeant Wilkins," Bill replied as he responded to the command.

There was a lull in the conversation as the sound of clinking forks scraped the bottom of the tins to retrieve all of the contents. The rations were sufficient enough for a small meal based on some starvation chart. Bishop could tell he was going to require a more sustaining diet and wondered if they had any candy bars tucked away somewhere.

The Captain was the first to split the sound of food being devoured, almost in unison.

"Sergeant Wilkins I've assigned the Corporal here to beacon duty. Clue him in please."

"Sir," Wilkins began swallowing hard. "He's just arrived, shouldn't he settle in first."

"I'm squared away Sergeant," Bishop commented to show he was on the job.

"None the less," Wilkins interjected. "You remember our snap message from Ottawa last month. We can expect increased bombing raids by the Americans."

"The Americans won't bomb in monsoon Sergeant," La Rouch said while taking in a mouth full of food. "Besides, Bishop should get his feet wet right away."

"But sir!" the Sergeant pleaded.

"Nope, see to it."

"Yes sir," Wilkins replied somewhat hesitantly. He always thought new men should have a little respite to acclimate to normal operations. "Be in the radio room at 8:45 Corporal."

"Right Sergeant." Bishop replied.

CHAPTER 5

It wasn't a room, but a walk-in closet that housed the electronics of the compound on the second floor. Across the hall from the doorway was a set of stairs that lead to the mansard roof of the château and where the signal dish sat directly in front of a large glass window. The window was the type normally seen in the artist lofts of Paris.

In a feeble attempt at camouflage a tarpaulin was draped over the dish like an artist would cover his painting on the easel. And equally apparent was the tarp didn't go all the way to the floor and the tripod legs holding the dish stuck out. It might have fooled someone if it wasn't for the rounded shape of the dish making the tarp look like an advertisement for a pregnant Frisbee.

"You're here," Wilkins said when he noticed Bishop standing in the doorway.

"As ordered."

Wilkins was adjusting a small transmitter dial, making sure it was zeroed in on the right frequency. To the right and covered by an inverted cardboard box was the teletype machine. It was their only connection to the embassy because the telephones in Hanoi were constantly breaking down due to the age of the equipment.

Moreover, the telephone lines themselves were a massive tangle of wires hanging from poles that shorted out during the slightest hint of rain. It was only during summer when storms were least threatening that most of the city could talk to each other.

Around the walls of the closet were hung old clothes and towels to make it appear as if the closet was more of a trash dump then a space used for messaging.

There was a single light bulb that hung on a cord from the center of the tiny room and it illuminated more of the hallway than the compartment.

This whole procedure was created by a previous Group leader when the system was first installed. In the beginning it was deemed okay to have the beacon, then he was told they couldn't have it so it had to be disguised as something else, then he was told that it may or may not be okay for it to be displayed. The only outcome was the Group leader ended up being a raving stark staring paranoid schizophrenic.

It was then that Bishop took a moment to observe the older man with three chevrons on his sleeve.

Sergeant Wilkins was completely familiar with the attitudes of defeat. He once served before his Canadian service, with the Tenth Parachute Regiment of the French Army in Algeria. He had witnessed first-hand the barbarism of colonial forces in the port town of Oran, and he too was a misplaced adventurer.

"Good to see you in summer dress," Wilkins commented.

"Yea, I was lucky John had an extra set."

"I think I can get you a couple of extra sets in a day or two. I know Sergeant Pogozinski.

"Pogo what?"

"Pogozinski, he's with the Polish contingent across town. There here to watch us and were here to watch them. So knowing this makes it easier if we trade stuff occasionally."

"Nice, saves money on bat scopes."

"Right, and so here is your duty," Wilkins began while pointing to a display on the face of what looked like a small TV set.

The next few moments were spent showing Bishop how to switch on and off, fine tune the transmitter and watch the wave length in the small TV screen. It was all very simple due to the fact the designers knew the average IQ of the operators wouldn't be much over that of a manhole cover.

When Bishop was comfortable with the new instructions for operation they both went up to the attic where the dish was.

"Now you take off the canvass and be careful to not knock the dish out of direction," Wilkins said as he gradually lifted the concealment of the transmitting device.

Bishop took hold of the canvass to assist with the removal and noticed the inner side was covered with silver paint of some kind.

"What the hell is this for?" Bishop said pointing at the shiny coating.

"It's so the North can't find our dish. The paint keeps any signal from going out if the transmitter down stairs is switched on accidently."

"Got it."

"Now after you get the cover off be sure that this switch is on," Wilkins said pointing to a small toggle device underneath the dish.

"Won't it work with it off?"

"No," replied Wilkins, his tone was imperious. Wilkins glanced at his watch it was a few minutes before nine PM. "Okay we'll leave it on and you can shut down at two AM."

"Five hours, so what do I do until then?"

Strolling casually toward the stairs down the Sergeant said with a grin, "You do what all good soldiers do, wait!"

"I've heard of walk'en a post in the boonies, but this is got to be the shits," Bishop replied as he went over to the only window and sat cross legged on the floor.

"Got to be the what?"

"Got to be the shits eh, Sergeant!"

"There's hope for you yet, Corporal." Wilkins replied with an unseen wink in the darkness of the room.

Bishop looked out the window into the darkness that hung like a glove on the roofs of the surrounding buildings. It had begun to rain and the drops looked like diamonds stuck to the pains. In the shadows of the garden below, he made out a small shape carrying something under his shirt, slipping over the wall.

CHAPTER 6

The last word in most Webster's Dictionaries is zymurgy, generally meaning the chemistry of fermentation. With a lack of alcohol being mostly confiscated by the local customs officer the Privates were forced to microbrew their own vintage of cabbage wine.

As Bishop stepped out onto the veranda the unmistakable scent of boiled cabbage met him and like a smack he was transported back to a Saint Patrick's Day party that was never to be forgotten. Everything was green even the jungle, but the corn beef was terrific.

"Morning Corporal," John said as he pulled the blue pickup truck to halt at the foot of the stairs.

"Yea John, where's the Sergeant?"

"Right behind you!"

Bishop turned quickly on his heel and came face to face with the NCO.

"I trust you turned off the beacon last night precisely at two?" Wilkins asked with the firmness of a landlord demanding last month's rent.

"Well, it wasn't two but close enough for Government work."

Wilkins stood inches from the Corporals face, his breath brushed at Bishops lips. "It's not so important at what time it goes off, as long as it's on at the appropriate hour."

"Right Sergeant, I won't forget."

"Best not, now get in and let's go."

Wilkins sat in the same place as La Rouch had done the day before with Bishop bunched between.

The day was overcast but clear, a steady wind from the east made curtain of it. It was just after morning coffee break and the markets weren't open yet. This made navigating the narrow streets much easier.

The truck bounced over the cobble stoned thoroughfares that need major renovation if one was going to keep from exploding his kidneys. Buildings looked poised to collapse and leafless trees lined the sidewalks. Everywhere just a few feet apart were inverted sewer pipes buried in the muddy earth forming make shift bomb shelters. For the most part the city seemed as rude as the weather.

"Bishop slouched as much as could be possible in the restricted cab and asked casually, "Ah Sergeant are those French Parachute wings you're wearing over your pocket?"

"Half size, yes."

"I didn't think we were allowed to wear foreign awards. I've got a set of jump wings too."

"But yours are from the American service right?"

"Yea so?"

"The French were defeated here long ago," Wilkins said as he looked to his right at something that took his attention momentarily. "And the North looks at it as a badge of disgrace."

"So why do you wear them?"

"To remind me that I have always done my duty, even when it was very unpleasant at the time."

"But you're not old enough to have been here in the fifties are you?"

"NO, I was in Algeria."

"With the Legion?"

"Part of it, yes."

"Damn, you guys kicked butt over there didn't yea?"

"Yes, for a while."

"How did it turn out?"

"Only history well tell. Now put on your arm badge were going into the airport."

Bishop noticed he hadn't pulled on the blue arm band with the globe and leaf pattern boldly displayed. It was their pass to just about anywhere in the country, but Bishop didn't know that yet.

Like the rest of the country and the day before, the airport terminal and tarmac were the same. The mostly sandy colored concrete runway worn by time, and sagging with small pools of water where everywhere. A gray curtain of mist surrounded the facility and it was nearly impossible to see the radio towers downtown.

After their check at the main gate John brought the truck around onto the tarmac where three planes were parked. Two were Chinese military aircraft, the cargo types and the second was painted all white with the Canadian flag displayed on the tail. It was a DE Havilland Dove, a short twin engine passenger plane that when the seats are removed makes a practical freight carrier.

John brought the truck to a stop near the cargo doors which were already open. An Air Force sergeant was standing by the short ladder that hung down for access. Through the doors the UN soldiers could see their supplies waiting for off–loading.

The three climbed from the truck and proceed to make transfer arrangements.

"Corporal you and John get to it, and I'm going into check with airport security," Wilkins ordered.

Bishop gave a half salute and joined John by the aircraft doors. The truck was close enough to the plane that the Air Force sergeant could toss the supplies down to John while Bishop kept track with the requisition order.

Nearly half the supplies had been transferred to the truck when John noticed Lieutenant Ho Buc standing by the tail gate. The Vietnamese officer scanned the contents while John stood looking on. Bishop had for some unknown reason walked up to the front of the plane and stood looking at the pilot's compartment window.

John knew what the officer wanted and turning snatched up a cardboard case that had cigarettes stenciled to the side. It was the total allotment for Group 6 for the next week, but it was also the customary payoff for Ho Buc's turning a blind eye.

Not that a blind eye was necessary, but on occasion a small wooden box with the word gin pasted on the side slipped through. Alcohol wasn't banded from the approved list of supplies to the embassy and the groups, but it was a very nice thing to trade on the black market which flourished better than the bombs that landed on it.

The officer smiled when handed the box and turned casually and headed for the office in the terminal building.

"JOHN!" Bishop called as he approached. "What did the fuck'en dink want?"

"His cut, what else."

Bishop pulled up beside his associate and they both looked in the direction Buc had gone.

"What cut?"

"He gets our cigs and sells them downtown. That way he doesn't bother us when we check out at the gate eh?"

"Shit, nothing changes," Bishop said as he started off in the direction of the terminal. "Two more boxes and were done Corp!"

"I'll be right back."

John smiled wryly; he knew the look of a man with a mission. Bishop not only had cause but justice was hopefully going to prevail.

John finished loading the last two boxes and then climbed into the cab, starting the motor instantly. Looking over he spotted Bishop entering the terminal.

It was at this very juncture that Wilkins had finished with his duties in the security office and was stepping through the door when he spotted the blue pickup headed straight for him.

"What's the rush, where's Bishop?" Wilkins said climbing into the passenger seat.

"Sergeant, he's about to start World War three," John said as he accelerated and drove to the other end of the terminal.

Inside the facility Bishop spotted Ho Buc standing beside a counter with his right arm holding the box of cigarettes. The officer was surprised by Bishop's presence and the other four guards rose from their chairs in response.

"What you want GI?"

Bishop said nothing and walked straight up to the officer. Without any trigger of anticipation, Bishop slapped the officer nearly knocking him down.

"Where the hell do you think you are Saigon?" Bishop screamed!

But before his words slipped into obscurity the guards had drawn their pistols and surround Bishop, being careful to not lay hands on him.

Busting through his armed cordon, Bishop grabbed up the box from the counter and screamed, "This belongs to us, NOT you, you little shit!"

"You soldier, attention," a voice blurted out like a fog horn from a distant reef.

"SIR!" Ho Buc called to his superior. "This man hit me down. He under arrest" Buc said as he yanked his pistol from its holster around his waist.

The Colonel descended a flight of stairs from a balcony office overlooking the waiting area. Dressed in a freshly starched uniform the Colonel joined the others being sure to stay behind his cordon of guards.

"Not yet he isn't," Wilkins called as entered the room.

Bishop suddenly began to feel like Custer just after all those Indians showed up. What looked like a skirmish was about to become an incident with diplomatic proportions.

"I see your man hit the lieutenant, Sergeant,' the collar tabs indicated the rank of Colonel in the North's Army.

"I beg to differ sir! He wasn't hit he was slapped. And as you know sir, there's a difference." Wilkins said.

"Yes," the Colonel responded in a serious tone. "But why was he slapped?" The Colonel's english was superior to the younger officer's indicating he had been educated some place besides the Hanoi Polytec.

"He's stealing our cigarettes sir," Bishop said.

"The Colonel's eyes glared at the Lieutenant. "Holster your weapon," the Colonel ordered.

"But sir, he break law. Not supposed to have contraband."

"It isn't contraband sir. We have it on our list approved by your ministry," Wilkins said as he snapped his fingers expecting Bishop to turn out the requisition form.

Bishop set the box back on the counter and began to search his pockets.

"Where is it Corporal?"

"I think it's still in the truck sergeant."

"It's not necessary," The Colonel said. "I know what you are to get every time that plane lands here."

The Colonel signaled to the guards to return to their duties. He then pointed a finger to Ho Buc and then redirected it in the direction of his office. The Lieutenant complied without retort.

"I will have to make a report on this," Sergeant. "Too many witnesses."

"Yes sir," Wilkins said and a low tone. It was if the two were conducting their own peace talks.

"You do realize sir that this has been going on for a while?"

"Yes sergeant," The Colonel said as he reached up and tugged at the upper button of his tunic.

"But that isn't for me to decide. I think you should take your Corporal and leave now."

"Yes sir," Wilkins replied and with a snap salute the confrontation had ended.

Wilkins and Bishop left, the case of cigarettes firmly tucked in the Corporal's arms. Outside it had started to rain as the truck with the three Canadians made for the front gate, and their quarters a few miles away.

CHAPTER 7

The ride back to the Old French Quarter where Group 6 was barrack was, somewhat like the weather, dreary. Neither man spoke a word as they each considered the trouble they might be in.

Questions of what rules were broken, how to make it seem like a storm in a tea cup sort of thing ruminated like old socks in Sergeant Wilkins mind. He had been on the job for more than a year and knew how minor incidents can either get blown out of proportion, or completely forgotten until next time.

Bishop knew that a slap in the face was more of an insult than striking someone out right. He had learned that when he was assigned to an ARVN unit in the South. He carried no remorse for the action, yet wondered if he would get away with it.

Most occurrences like this one was allocated to the expression, 'guess what the fucking new guy did?' type of chatter that traveled like black smoke throughout the unit.

John seemed to be day dreaming as he guided the truck down the wide boulevard. He was more apprehensive about the burning of the cabbage while they were gone. Wine with a hint of blistered vegie as a back flavor didn't sit well on the palate, especially after six or eight glasses of the inadequate stuff.

Drifting past the south end of Bi Mau Lake, which was part of Lenin Park, Bishop could just make out the formal steps that sat of the bank to the north. Once several decorative white plaster buildings served as a rest stop for walkers along the lakes edge, but were now merely bombed out craters.

Just over the darkened tree tops was the three hundred foot flag pole with the North's colors the size of large house hanging from it. The wet flag looked like a drowning man clinging to the only remaining flotation device that wasn't waterlogged.

Bicycle traffic along the streets was picking up. The groups of shanties that occupied the sidewalks were beginning to show life. Some of the squatters who had lost their houses during air raids in the outlying areas were even sweeping the space in front of their soggy accommodations.

The blue pickup arched around a traffic director dressed in camouflage and puttered up Mi Hac De street, formerly known as Petain Terrace when the French had their own traffic cop stationed on the corner.

A few minutes further on ended with a right turn into Group 6 compound. The truck rolled to a stop in front of the garage as the three dismounted. Wilkins ordered Ed, who was tending the garden to join with John to unload the truck.

Snatching a carton of Players cigarettes from the cardboard box, Wilkins ordered Bishop to his quarters until further notice, which he suggested won't be long in coming.

Wilkins reported to Captain La Rouch's office and quarters that were combined in the same room.

Somewhat larger than the other rooms in the chateau, the Captain had organized his space into segments that overlapped each other. Sleeping occupied the south corner of the room, his desk and maps of the city took up most of the western boarder while a sitting area near the only window was on the north side.

The view out the window was blocked by the compound wall that surrounded the facility. On the outside barrier there was a hand painted rendering of a garden that had been faded by the elements. The former owners felt a desire to have something to look at besides white plaster.

When Sergeant Wilkins nocked on the oak door it was answered by a forceful 'enter.'

Wilkins brought himself to attention and made the customary salute to the Captain who was leaning back in his chair as if he was contemplating the future of the world.

"Sir," Wilkins began taking off his dark blue beret and flinging it with one motion under his left arm. The precision maneuver spoke of years of practice.

La Rouch's eyes went full bean when he spotted the cigarette carton and asked while leaning forward, "Are those real?"

"Yes sir," Wilkins replied as he sat the package down on the desk.

La Rouch swooped up the box and ripped into it like he had found the missing part of a lottery ticket.

"How did you get it past that damned Lieutenant at the airport?"

"Well sir, "Wilkins said while starring at the pack of cigarettes the Captain had finished opening. "Can I have one of those?"

La Rouch handed him the pack and Wilkins extracted one of the rollups, placing the smoke between his lips the Captain offered a light from his small Bic lighter.

The two men drew on their smokes as if they hadn't seen one in months. In fact it truly had been that long.

"You were saying Sergeant?" La Rouch said like someone tasting a fine wine.

"Oh yes sir," Wilkins began as he regained his military demeanor. "This is our good news for the day sir."

"Oh," La Rouch said curiously. It was the kind of response the Captain typically gave when he was about to be bulldozed into oblivion. "And I take it there's other news of the day?"

"Well yes sir. It seems Mr. Bishop has been indoctrinated into our belligerent's customs of non-aggression."

"God it's good to have one of these again," La Rouch said as he inhaled another lung full of smoke. He starred at the cigarette like it was a pen that could write upside down.

"Better than those Bolshevik firecrackers we've been smoking," Wilkins replied thoughtfully.

"How did you get them through?"

"It wasn't me sir it was Bishop."

"Bishop, what the hell has he got to do with it?"

"It seems Corporal Bishop has a knack for getting what he wants by way of gentle persuasion."

"How gentle?"

"Well, it's like this sir," Wilkins began and after a few minutes of reporting events and a summation of what might be overly stated as an act of war, the Sergeant rested his case.

"Good God," La Rouch replied. "The man hasn't been here one day and already he's up to it eh."

"He does have talent in that direction sir."

"I guess that's what they want me up at the embassy for."

"Front office wants you sir."

"Of course. I got the message of the teletype about ten minutes ago. I thought by the way Major Tennyson was talking it was about one of my reports. But I guess this must be the reason."

"What time will you need the truck sir," Wilkins asked casually.

"Have it out front by three fifteen. It shouldn't take more than ten minutes to get over there."

"Right sir," Wilkins replied and snuffed out his half smoked cigarette in the clean ashtray on the desk.

"By the way, I guess you ought to have Bishop drive. I'll give him directions."

"Right."

"And make out your SS 24 report. It might have something in it that will keep them from shipping me off to count Caribou on Baffin Island."

"Yes sir," Wilkins replied giving a quick salute and exiting the office.

CHAPTER 8

The enlisted man's club was typically off limits to NCO's like Bishop. But after being released from house arrest, or what might be consider such by an officer of the regular army, he made his way to the machine shed to see what John and Ed were up to.

The intense odor of the boiling cabbage grew steadily as Bishop approached the rattled structure. All the windows had been properly boarded up except for one that had an exquisite view of the courtyard. If one needed a vantage point of observe the comings and goings of the rated ranks this window was perfect for the job.

What was unusual about the building was it made the corner of the surrounding wall. It was as if the former builders considered it to be a square bastion and serve as a rear defensive position. Then someone decided to put a roof on it and make it a garden shed. But that was before the lower echelon members of the Canadian contingent arrived and needed a place to hide the still.

Stepping through the doorway Bishop paused as he spotted Ed and John huddled around a coil of copper tubing.

"One of you guys should be watching this place when you're doing that," Bishop announced.

Like two deer realizing their impending doom by an oncoming truck the men snapped to attention. The metal canteen cup Ed was holding dropped to the floor and small puddle began to collect around it. The contents, a syrupy substance slipped out as it too was being condemned.

"Sorry Corporal," John said.

"Yea, we didn't know you were around eh," Ed commented almost apologetically.

"Well I am, and I'd rather be in here than out there."

"What's up?" Ed asked.

"I told you, he belted Ho Buc at the airport this morning," John said.

"I didn't belt him, I slapped him," Bishop said as he walked over and seated himself on a small barrel. "There's a difference okay."

"Okay sure Corporal, I hope they see it that way." Ed replied as he turned and snatched up the canteen cup and put it under the end of the copper tube to collect the drippings.

It was an unspoken suggestion that once the formal amenities were exercised that a sense of casual air settled between the three. As all soldiers learn, camaraderie is the engine for a respected friendship.

"Well I'll find out latter I guess," Bishop began as he reached over and felt the side of the boiling pot. It looked like it wasn't hot enough to help move the process of distillation along.

"The CO wants me to drive him to the embassy this afternoon."

"Hey! You're probably going to see Sam, give him this ten dong I owe him," John said slipping the monetary note from his pants pocket.

"Who the hell is Sam?" Bishop asked.

"Oh you'll know Sam. He's got what we can't get most of the time," Ed replied.

"Like what?"

"Money," John answered. "He's got his hand in a bank somewhere," John chortled.

"Why? Don't we get paid around here?"

"Sure, but it don't last long."

"It never does," Bishop said with contempt. He knew all too well that members of the military were always under paid.

Running his finger under the end of the copper tubing Bishop felt a hot drop land on the end of it. Bring it up to his lips he licked it.

"God!" Bishop barked, the taste was horrifyingly awful. "You don't drink this stuff do you?"

The two other soldiers chuckled in a proud way. They had the right flavor for their consumption.

"What else we going to do with it?" John asked wryly.

"You could polish anchor chains with it," Bishop said as he rose and walked toward the exit. "Keep your eyes open from now on okay?"

"Right Corporal," John replied as Bishop left the room.

"Yep," Ed said matter-of-factly. "He'll be back."

CHAPTER 9

The sprinkled rain had stopped long enough for a slip of sun light to wash over the compound as Bishop and Captain La Rouch headed for the embassy. The blue pickup looked clean with the mist that fell earlier and had yet to dry.

Like campers on holiday the two Canadian's drove out the gate of the compound and headed east toward the Red River only fifteen blocks away. It wouldn't take long for them to go the mile and a half to headquarters of the ICC that was formerly a lavish hotel. The resort was once used by the French Freedom Council as their head office, until they were run out.

What seemed odd was the location of the offices was on the north side of the Old Quarter and there was no direct route to the building. Large vehicle travel through the Old Quarter was nearly impossible except for motorized rickshaws. The streets were so narrow that house to house fighting by the Legionnaires' was more like room to room.

Bishop kept a steady pace with cycle traffic making sure not to get too close to a potential mishap which could cost the Canadian government a large sum in restitution. A month's salary wasn't much in Corporals pay, but in the North's currency it was a hefty windfall to the injured.

"I guess I really screwed up sir?" Bishop said to break the silence.

"Just one thing I need to be certain about?" La Rouch replied as he opened a brown folder on his lap. It was the only brief case available to the small contingent.

"What's that sir?"

"Sergeant Wilkins reports that after you hit the Lieutenant he drew his gun right?"

"I didn't hit him sir I slapped him."

"I don't see the distinction."

"Well sir, if you slap a dink that's an insult. If you hit him you're in for it."

"And where did you learn that?"

"Down South."

La Rouch paused as he weighed the difference wondering how much of a disparity could be garnered from such an action of force.

"But he drew his gun on you right?"

"Oh yes sir!"

"Good, that should keep from counting Caribou for a while."

"Caribou sir?"

"Inside joke Corporal, turn left here," la Rouch ordered when they reached the river front road.

Bishop obeyed and slid into the next current of traffic. But once on the main boulevard although much wider it was also more crowded.

What caught Bishop's eye was that it looked a lot like the road along the Perfume River in Hue. There was a broad grassy space between the road and the river bank and it was studded with half dead Beatle nut trees.

Scattered along the way were old derelict French Army trucks with holes in them the size of trash can lids. On each vehicle were bundles of bamboo in the shape of missiles. The simulated rockets were green and had red stars painted on them.

"Are you believe'n that?" Bishop said with a grin.

"What?"

"Check out those trucks with the rockets on them. You got to be kidding me Jack, that wouldn't stop a fast mover from lighting them up."

"They're for air defense and are non-lethal."

"Oh come on sir, if that don't bring the Navy downtown nothing will."

"Then the US would be the belligerent aggressor and will be written up appropriately."

"But the dinks are suck 'in us in with that shit."

"It's irrelevant. Target identification is of the upmost importance."

"Not at Mach 1 it ain't," Bishop replied jokingly.

Bishop began to simmer with resentment. Here he was in a military unit that couldn't shoot back and could get clobbered from either side and all he could do is write a report. In a moment of extreme frustration he vowed his reports would be filled with all the facts and not what could be seen from a passing truck.

La Rouch pointed out they were nearing the embassy that lay just beyond the bridge crossing the river to the village of Bat Trang, the old railroad bridge was a half mile farther on.

By the time they got to the bridge entry a traffic cop brought the boulevard circulation to a halt. With hands waving like he was trying to put out a fire with a wet rope, the signalman hastened the onslaught of travellers onto the bridge.

"Man this looks like 52nd and Park at about two thirty." Bishop said surveying the sea of cross traffic.

It was then that La Rouch was struck by the existence of the Corporal whose military experience included service down south. For some strange reason he didn't consider such an asset of intelligence just sitting there like a bent door knob. It was as if a blinding flash of the obvious swooped in and landed squarely on his shoulders.

It was now time for La Rouch to see if Bishop could shed light on a problem that had come his way. Something that he had been in hot water with his superiors for several months but was unable to conclude, or at least get some decent evidence to back up his query to the higher ups.

For more than a month the Captain had been carrying with him a thirty dollar note in a currency he hadn't seen before. He had found it when searching a small house near an unexploded bomb site on the far-east side of the city. It was stuck to the bottom of a rice bag that had been knocked over by someone trying to leave in a hurry.

Reaching into the back pocket of his dark blue sorts the Captain retrieved his wallet. Opening it, he dug around for the tightly folded note that he kept hidden in the lining. With two slender fingers he removed the note and gently unfolded it making sure Bishop was looking on.

"Corporal, have you ever seen something like this?"

Bishop smiled and reached over for the piece of currency that was no bigger than two business cards. He instantly recognized it but then something curious drew his attention, it was what was not there that made him ask, "Yes sir, but where did you get this?"

"That doesn't matter now. What is it?"

"Well its MPC, military payment currency. It's what we used down south to pay for stuff."

"I thought that was what it was."

"It says it here right on the back," Bishop said as he turned the note over. It was then that he noticed there was no such writing on the note.

"That's weird," Bishop said. "Our stuff usually said it, but this doesn't have it. It's got the MPC in big letters on the front and the picture of the rice paddies but on the back there's no mention of what it is."

"But you can see it's a thirty dollar note?"

"Yes sir, but that's another thing. I don't remember ever seeing a thirty dollar bill."

"But that doesn't mean they didn't have any?"

"No sir it doesn't, but all our stuff was in US denominations like ones, fives, tens, and so on. We don't have thirty dollar bills."

"Right," La Rouch said retrieving the certificate and neatly sliding it back into the seclusion of his wallet.

"So where did you get from sir?"

"I found it," the Captain replied in a secretive manner. "Okay, we can go now."

Bishop checked the sides of the truck for any hangers on and then moved forward with the rush of other travellers.

A few blocks on Bishop turned down a narrow street and spotted their destination. The hotel was on the right and distinguished by a Canadian flag hanging at a forty five degree angle over the arched entry. Beyond the arch was the inner courtyard, the only off street parking available.

CHAPTER 10

Within minutes of Bishop and the Captain leaving the compound Sergeant Wilkins came out to the small three stall garage and opened the large wooden door to one of the bays. It was dark inside the garage for deliberate reasons. Added to the poor light was a cluttering of odds and ends piled up nearly to the ceiling. This made it hard to see what was stored away in the corners and insured the secrets of being kept.

This particular bay had a small wooden cart in it, the type used by street peddlers and it contained a set of tires and several cardboard boxes of auto parts. The Sergeant grabbed the sturdy handles and hauled the cart out into the yard and set it next to the garden plot.

Wilkins returned to the bay and in the back swung a heavy green tarp off of small car. The Russian made Lada was in reasonably good shape and in warm weather ran fairly well.

Opening the hood Wilkins retrieved a hammer off a nearby bench and swung it with malice striking the motor on the top of the flywheel. The sound of a gasp emanated and that signaled Wilkins to try and start the motor.

This practice was important because whenever the engine was switched off and the car sat for a long time the cylinders would hold the compression and starting was nearly impossible. The gasping sound was the release of the compression as the engine made a half turn and paused.

Wilkins slammed the hood shut, hopped in and turned the switch. The engine sputtered to life as a cloud of blue smoke poured out the back like a defense mechanism. He then reached inside the glove box and withdrew two important items. The maroon colored beret with Polish airborne wings on the front, and a small flag of Poland.

The Sergeant put on the beret and with a single tug pulled the cover into a perfect fit. Its previous owner had carefully shaped the hat after years of wear to conform immediately upon settlement to the head. He then stepped from the car and slid the small flag into a hole drilled in the center of the hood.

With license plates of the Polish government and the small flag combined with his red beret he was certain to not be stopped by the Gray Mice, the North's Secret Police.

It was common knowledge that the three nations of Poland, Hungary, and Canada were playing the role of observers, but it was also understood that only the Canadians had to have a travel pass to get around.

The gray mice were always watching the occupants of cars. The Polish with their red berets, the Hungarians and their tan berets were rarely stopped. But the Canadian's with their dark blue berets were a perfect target for search and seizure.

Backing the small black car out of its den Wilkins stopped by the front steps of the chateau.

"BILL!" Wilkins called out.

The Sergeant didn't have to wait long when the Private First appeared on the porch.

"Yes Sergeant," Bill replied

"Stay by the phone, if anyone calls say we're all over at the embassy."

"And if anyone asks for you?"

Pausing to think of an untraceable reply, Wilkins called back, "Tell them on a mail run."

"Right Sergeant!" Bill replied and hustled back inside the building heading straight for his room on the second floor.

Climbing into his bunk he graded a copy of the Toronto Sun and fumbled through the sports section. His room was only a few feet from the small communications room and the ding of the telex would notify him on any messages being sent from the embassy.

Wilkins laid on the gas and the smoking Lada bolted from the compound gate and sliced its way into traffic with the vengeance of a crouching tiger.

The first thing Wilkins had learned was that Pol's weren't very good drivers. He felt that changing that tradition would attract attention by the gray mice. Posing as a Warsaw Pack national would be very uncomfortable for him, if ever caught at it.

As the Sergeant headed down the narrow street in the direction of Lenin Park he laughed to himself when thinking about how he had acquired his unauthorized mode of transportation. The Polish sergeant he was going to meet with had given it to him as a prize. Not that Wilkins had won anything, but it helped to have the Canadian's overlook an event which happened a year earlier.

Sergeant Pogozinski had been in service as long as Wilkins and had written off the car just before its return to the homeland, claiming it had been totaled by a land mine. For the most part, Lada's were considered a write off the minute they rolled off the assembly line. The beret and flag were also a gift.

In a way Pogozinski was burning the candle at both ends. His job was to report violations to the United Nations via Warsaw and Moscow, and yet he had several family members employed at the Arco Steel plant in Hamilton Ontario. Loyalty was a tricky thing when you're on the wrong side, and to him, he felt he had always been on the wrong side. Especially when he received the occasional letter from family living in a democratic country of how much better it is just getting to the food store.

Wilkins parked his official looking car near the corner of Tri Bang and Do Ha streets. On the northern corner of the intersection was a bar that was frequented by the Pol's and Russian advisors to the North. It was called the Krakow Club. Not much of a place but it had an interior that gave some solace to the foreign countrymen who visited it regularly.

On the opposite corner was the northern most part of Lenin Park. Formerly the city dump, it was back filled in the early 1960's in honor of the Soviet leader, and some trees were planted. Parts of vehicles and rubber tires broke the soil in most places and hardly any grass grew. Along the shoreline old fisher man still clung to the hope of catching the one that keeps getting away.

Wilkins didn't bother to lock the vehicle mostly because it was extremely embarrassing when he couldn't open the door for a month while the tumblers reset themselves.

Dressed very much like a Polish soldier Wilkins made for the pub. He knew that Pogozinski and some of his friends would be at the watering hole usually about the same time.

The interior of the Club was bleak and Spartan in décor. White walls had been faded by time and pictures of Lenin, Stalin and Ingles were prominently hung behind the bar as if they were counting the dong slipping under the tables. A few lamps were center piece of a well abused collection of tables for the gusts, and a long bench like affair made for larger gatherings, held court along the back wall. It was this seating arrangement that was presently the object of the Polish contingent's control.

Wilkins entered through the small doorway and paused long enough for his eyes to get accustomed to the dim lighting. But it wasn't necessary to see where he was going. The Pol's were singing a course of an old Russian airborne song they learned in Soviet jump school.

"Haw, if it isn't the lost Canook," Pogozinski shouted upon seeing Wilkins approaching the group. "Sit here and you can join us. We'll protect you my friend."

Wilkins maneuvered toward the forceful frame of the commanding NCO. He took a seat on the bench and glanced to make sure he knew everyone. It was a habit to notice anyone new to the group.

"Don't let me interrupt the festivities Pogozinski, "Wilkins said as he motioned with his hands to get the second course going again.

As if orchestrated by the great Ludwig, the other four NCO's began to sing again, only this time much louder. It was good cover for what Wilkins wanted to talk to his friend about.

Leaning in toward the Polish Sergeant Wilkins, not wanting to be over heard muttered his request.

"I need a favor and I can't pay for it."

"You know Sergeant Wilks," Pogozinski began. He had a habit of not pronouncing the Canadian's full last name. It wasn't out of disrespect, he just liked Wilks better.

"If you insist on wearing our hat you should just save time and come over to our way."

"Are you kidding? The paper work would strangle me."

"Da!" Pogozinski said with a grin. "But what a coupe."

Wilkins smiled and nodded. He knew all too well what diplomatic upheaval there would be if a defection were in the cards.

"About my problem eh?"

"Yes, yes," Pogozinski said leaning in as if to mimic his counterpart.

"I need a couple of pairs of your shorts, about a 38 waist."

"Used of course?"

"Of course."

"And by when?"

"A few days."

"Problem solved. Supply is sending home old stock tomorrow; I'll hook in a couple pair for you. Anything else?"

"Yea, have you heard anything more about the warehouse out at the airport?"

"The one with the printing presses?"

"Yup, that be the one."

"No, but I think," Pogozinski paused. His eyes widened at the two Soviet Officers of the NKVD who just entered the room looking for a table.

"Oh damn," Wilkins whispered as he glanced over his shoulder and spotted the same two men.

"You get going now."

"Right."

Wilkins stood and walked toward the door with a sense of urgency. But before he could make it to the street one of the officers halted him in his tracks. He looked at the officer who was gazing at the French parachute wings he had forgotten to take off.

"It is alright comrade Captain. He is one of us. Mission important," Pogozinski called out over the din of the Russian song which had gotten two octaves higher.

The Officer nodded as Wilkins briskly gave a Polish salute as the custom warranted. Wilkins gesture was returned and he quickly stepped through the door and out onto the street.

To his surprise the Lada started and Wilkins was back at the compound in record time.

CHAPTER 11

L ike all hotels of early colonization this one was in better shape than most around the city. Perhaps because it laid within the confines of the old quarter that made it less of a target to bombers, or that it had no front steps to speak of.

Entry from the narrow street was through a Kragsyde style arch leading into a courtyard completely surrounded by three floors of spacious rooms. It was its overall appearance that made it look more like an office building than a hotel. Very little ornamentation remained to give the impression it once served Frances elite while on vacation to the orient.

Bishop guided the truck through the archway in the center of the building and found a space in the piazza near a portico which garnished a more distinctive entry. The brass doors had been polished recently, but the cold damp weather hand faded its gleam.

The two men slid from the truck and headed into the sanctum of the embassy.

Typical of the hotel floor plan, the main lobby had a separate door directly across from the one they had entered. It led to the street as well, and Bishop could see it had more of an attractive elegance to it than the one they had come through.

"They're on the second floor," La Rouch said as he turned to his left and headed for the circular stair case.

Bishop followed close behind and spent most of the short climb admiring the pretentiousness of the old structure. It was if he was in an architectural student on a field trip.

When they reached the spacious hall of the second floor La Rouch walked briskly to the office of the Embassy Adjutant which was at the far end of the building. Bishop dallied behind his eyes darting from side to side taking in all the familiarity of the business zone. The sound of typewriters clicking away filled the air and a musty redolence plucked the senses like an afterthought.

When the Captain entered the anteroom he paused before a small desk that blocked the doorway to the Major's outer office. A slick looking Corporal held the fort.

The Majors clerk was an older man with gray hair combed back over his head. His uniform was smart, recently starched and pressed. Falling out for morning formation was something he never had to do.

Bishop had followed his superior into the cramped space and closed the door taking up a defensive position in the corner. What was odd was there were no other chairs in the room and it left the impression one didn't have long to wait.

"You can go straight in Captain, the boss is waiting," the clerk said firmly.

"I was afraid of that," La Rouch replied and swung around the desk into the outer office closing the door behind him.

Suddenly the room fell silent, like the shock wave of an exploding bomb dissipating leaving the survivor shaken, but not stirred.

"So you're the yank from Ottawa," the clerk said as he kept his eyes trained on some form that needing filling out.

Bishop shifted his weight, not sure how to respond. He knew he wasn't in familiar waters and that made things extremely duplicitous.

"I see you've been issued summer dress, that isn't in your file."

"Yea well it's borrowed," Bishop replied.

"Very resourceful, for someone like yourself."

Bishop's curiosity got the better of him as he took up residence in front of the desk. Watching to see if the clerk looked up or not, Bishop imposed of sense of nervousness on the clerk when he snatched the name plate from its perch beside the out basket.

"Oh, Corporal Samuel Atwater. I don't believe we have been introduced?"

"Rather pointless at this juncture." Sam said, still not looking up. He then held a form out in front of him, and like a butterfly landing on a flower, he lowered the form down into the out basket.

"What did you mean about that resourceful crap?"

"I've obviously read your file. I make a point to know everyone's business. It may come in handy someday," Sam remarked now focused on another form.

"I think I know who you are," Bishop began cleverly as if he had just solved the case of the missing diamonds. "You're the pay-dog."

"The WHAT?" Sam responded and this time he did look up with furious eyes.

Bishop smirked. "Don't get excited, every unit's got one."

"Got WHAT?"

"The guy that makes payday loans." Bishop said.

Sam replanted himself more firmly in his swivel chair and turned his attention back to the form on his desk. He wasn't use to being on the defensive. When you're holding another man's marker you always have the upper hand of the situation. Especially when you have a genuine officer rank to call on for support.

"From time to time it becomes necessary to extend a bit of credit to your fellow enlistees. Our pay vouchers can go astray and it's good policy to not piss off the guy who can find it for you," Sam remarked keeping his eyes from making contact with his new adversary.

"You got that right Corporal," Bishop said with a grin.

"I think it might be best if you waited some where's else."

"Okay," Bishop said as he eased toward the door. "I'll be down stairs with the rest of the Remington Raiders."

"Finnnne," Sam replied extending the emphasis like a snake cautioning its next meal.

"Oh," Bishop said as he pulled the ten dong note from his shirt pocket. "This is from John at Group 6; he says he owes you this."

"I know who John is," Sam said as he snatched the cash from Bishops hand.

Bishop held tightly to the note, as Sam tried to pry it louse. "Don't I get a receipt?"

"It's a gentleman's agreement thank you very much," Sam replied firmly still trying to get his money.

Bishop relinquished his hold on the note and added, "Then I guess all our agreements will be on the sly?"

"If you're lucky," Sam said then added. "Yank!"

Bishop slipped out and headed for the lobby. It would be safer, he thought if he was less visible by hiding amongst the other clerks.

*   *   *

Captain La Rouch was having a less amiable time of it sitting before the Adjutant, Major Tennyson. It was customary when officers met that they maintained a more managerial attitude, rather than commander to subordinate.

The Major's field of influence was over the contingent forces that included the entire outlying Group's, what few there were. Group 6 was downtown Hanoi, Group 2 was within a mile of the DMZ and Group 5 was in Haiphong Harbor. Haiphong saw the most action by the other belligerent party.

Tennyson rarely agreed with the Embassy Director's office and as such an imaginary wall of complete distrust existed between the two. So much so that whenever Ottawa sent a flash message it had to be acknowledged by both departments and the ramifications of such an order took weeks to determine. Then a second message had to be sent back to Ottawa confirming the actual intent so the two parties could come to some sort of agreement.

Tennyson was a rather stout man of six feet. The type of man when he sat down his waist size was a 38, but when he stood up it was 32. His grayish hair was always in need of a good trimming and his sleepy green eyes constantly searched through bushy eyebrows.

At the moment he was reading the reports the Captain had turned in along with the incident report supplied by Colonel Chin, the airport commander.

"And so your new Corporal has made some friends here has he?" Tennyson said looking up from the report.

"It would seem so sir," La Rouch replied nervously. "But I'm sure he was in the right."

"Not according to Chin he wasn't?"

"But sir, with all due respect to Colonel Chin, he is Chinese. They sent him her to spy on us."

"That information hasn't been verified officially."

"And do you think the Chinese are going to send us his resume?"

"Not likely, but I get your point," Tennyson said as he pulled another report in front of him.

It was hard for the Captain to read the Major. The Commander had a habit of keeping his head at a slightly lowered angle making it hard to see what his intensions were. Probably a practice he acquired dealing with politicians.

"Your Belligerent Provocation Infraction report needs a bit of polish if I'm going to accept it."

"How so sir?"

"Well Sergeant Wilkins says and I quote, 'at that moment the Lieutenant drew is gun.'"

"And what should it say sir?"

"Well something like the Lieutenant drew his revolver. It gives the sentence a more urgent ring to it."

"Gun, revolver, what difference does it make. They both mean the same thing."

"You're quite right technically, but for those in Ottawa and up the hall, it should sound more threating."

"Yes sir. And do you think there will be any repercussions from this?"

"I think not," The Major said leaning back in his chair. "Just take it back, do a rewrite and send it in. I'll make sure it lands on the Directors desk when he's away. Tuck it in with his junk mail. That way when he gets back and tosses out the mail he won't have read it and he'll be the one to roast. Not me. I'll have the duplicate with the date stamp."

The Captain grinned at the cleverness of his commander. He could tell he had a lot to learn before he'd be ready for station command.

"As for the Corporal, get him lost for a while."

"Lost sir?"

"Yes," the Major said as he reached inside his desk and pulled out another form. "This came in the other day, the North has shot down another American plane down by Group 2. Send the Corporal down to look it over. Make sure it's a recent shot down and not from last year."

"Yes sir."

"Those buggers would have got away with it had they washed the dust off the damn thing."

"I'll have him bring back a piece of it so we can substantiate the report."

"Yes, that will do nicely. Now," the Major began. "For the real reason I sent for you."

"Sir?"

Tennyson stuck a finger in his ear and twisted it a few times while scratching an itch. Then he began, "I have a response from Ottawa on your suggestions of counterfeit money."

"Really sir," La Rouch said while sitting on the edge of his chair.

"Don't get excited, you're not going to like it. I sent off your file to Ottawa and it came back yesterday."

The Major pulled a larger brown file from his upper desk drawer and dropped it on the flat surface before him. Grabbing the lower left corner he yanked the cover open and paused to read a short paragraph.

"In all five statements reviewed by this board and with no significant evidence to show due cause, it is the recommendation that no action be forth coming. Copies to you, Group 6, me and etcetera, etcetera."

"But the thirty dollar note I sent in. Surly that is due cause."

The Major pointed to the ceiling in a gesture to wait a minute. Sort of a eureka, I blew it again.

A few pages into the file he found another MPC note arrested by a paper clip. Tugging at it the Major produced the note and held it up.

"See, it's the same as the one you turned in."

"No it's not sir. That is a ten dollar note and the one I turned in was for thirty," the Captain said while reaching into his back pocket and hauling out his wallet. In a second the note he had showed Bishop was free from the confines and he handed it to Tennyson.

The Major looked at both forms of currency and then said, "The only difference I see is the denomination is different."

"Turn it over sir."

The Major complied and in an instant he noticed something was missing.

"You see sir," the Captain began. "The ten dollar note has the words, 'Military Payment Currency,' written on it just inside the boarder. The thirty dollar's doesn't have it."

"Yes, your right. But I would contend it wasn't put on there for reasons unknown to us."

"There's another thing sir," the Captain said. "Bishop served with the US forces down south and he says they never made a thirty dollar note. All the MPC was based on the same denominations as the green backs. It cut down on confusion with the GI's"

"I was really hoping we could put this to rest," the Major said with a sigh.

"Sir, if I could get a free travel pass I could probably find the stuff."

"I know, and every tip you get by the time you arrive you're a day late and a dollar short."

"Yes, now you understand sir?"

"All I know at this point is that Ottawa is hammering on it and the North keeps claiming we're working for the Americans. Until relations improve we're buggered."

La Rouch feel back in his chair as if he just finished the six minute mile unsuccessfully.

"By the way," the Major began. "This Bishop served with the US forces didn't he?"

"Yes sir."

"Then he's still a Canadian citizen eh?"

"Yes sir. Only his visa expired, not his loyalty."

"Why the hell they'd send him to us is beyond me. Some damn Liberal is probably having a good laugh at our expense," the Major concluded with contempt.

"Wait a minute," La Rouch said sitting up as if he was just bit in the ass by one of those nasty tiger mosquitoes. "How did that ten dollar note get in my file? I sent in a thirty dollar note with that report."

"Oh God," the Major proclaimed. He had one of those gotcha moments and it didn't feel like a pinch in the behind by a beautiful woman at a Champaign party. "I have a feeling we've been compromised."

"By who?"

"By whom, and I don't bloody know."

"So now what sir?"

"So now," the Major began as he took up the file and handed the thirty dollar note back to the Captain. "We put this in my top drawer and see what happens."

"Now long do we wait sir?"

"You go back to your unit and keep your eyes open," the major said while closing his desk drawer with the file in it. "And see if you can get a couple steps ahead of these jokers. If you know for sure of something that we can get our hands on then call me."

"About Bishop sir?"

"Yes, oh," the Major replied as he paused to consider the ramifications of having a former US employee hanging around a sensitive area like Hanoi. "Yes, there's a chopper headed up here for resupply to Group 2 tomorrow. It should be in about noon. Have Bishop stop by and collect his travel pass. And make damn sure he's on that helicopter."

The Major had already arranged Bishops passage earlier when he first got the report from Colonel Chin. He could see beyond that what lay in the fore front to what occupied the background, and that had its advantages.

"Yes sir," La Rouch said as he rose and gave a snappy salute.

The Captain was feeling better thinking his theory was still a possibility. Or at least someone other than himself thought so.

CHAPTER 12

La Rouch hadn't been emulsified by the futility of discovery. Unlike freshman politicians who come to government with this air of accomplishment, which eventually becomes unsustainable by the ever encroaching dogma of policy, La Rouch thought of himself more as a modern day Sherlock Homes. He had a longer lease on youth which in its own way produces a certain curiosity for the truth. Something he had to constantly struggle to get out of dishonest belligerents.

Bishop was standing in the lobby waiting for the Captain, in front of a sign with a red band around it. The band gave the impression to all who saw it that it contained a huge level of philosophical perception.

It looked like a banner at first but as Bishop got closer he noticed it was some kind of quote written in French.

"Ready Corporal, "La Rouch asked taking a position beside the slightly younger man.

"Ah, yes sir."

"Like what it says?"

"I don't know sir I can't read French."

"Didn't you study it in high school?"

"Yes sir. But that was French Canadian. This is real French."

The Captain assumed the role of educator and pointing with his finger as if conducting a sing along, he began, "What do we have that makes us think we're better than what we are?"

"Did some drunk write that?" Bishop queried."

"Hardly, the former owners wrote it just before they were kicked out of Vietnam."

"That's about right," Bishop said turning toward the door. "Another great expectation shot to hell."

"Well the North thinks it's apropos and won't let it be painted over."

"So we got to stare at this thing every time we come in here?"

"Afraid so."

"Are you ready sir?"

La Rouch nodded and the two tramped toward their transportation back to Group 6.

*   *   *

Bishop navigated the courtyard and made for the street, somewhat frustrated by the sign and its contents. The blue truck was like a beacon in the gray haze which feel from the overcast.

The Corporal always thought that hind sight can be very informative; it helps you to see the bricks coming at you. He never considered winners of ever having to look back. Besides, in most cases who enjoys contemplating train wrecks?

Once on the narrow street from which he had come the Corporal headed west hoping to beat rush hour traffic. Through the rain spotted windshield he could see the walls of the old Citadel at the far end. The leafless trees made for a fuzzy view but the stressed sandstone fort was unmistakable.

After passing through the first intersection without bashing into anyone Bishop noticed the street got wider. For once maneuvering was more like a convenience instead of a task.

It was then that a jeep carrying four gray mice rolled out from behind an oncoming rickshaw which caused Bishop to hit the brakes. The police seemed to be in a hurry to take such a chance to pass oncoming traffic in their direction.

Not stopping the jeep roared passed and then wheeled onto the sidewalk rolled back into the street to take up a tailing position behind the Canadians.

"Got our travel pass ready?" Bishop remarked as he eyes darted from the rear view mirror to the street ahead.

La Rouch glanced out the rear window of the cab and slumped back into his seat.

"Keep driving, we don't have anything to worry about as long as we look like we're headed in the right direction."

"I hope your right sir these guys look like they're about to shit in our Cheerios."

It was as if the Captain was clairvoyant, the trouble Bishop was expecting stayed right on their bumper until they turned into the compound at Group 6. Bouncing over the curb and rolling into the courtyard Bishop stopped in front of main door.

La Rouch paused before getting out. He looked over at the third stall of the garage and spotted the marks in the wet dirt where the door had been dragged open then closed. He instinctively knew that Sergeant Wilkins had been out in their shadow car. And for what reason he would learn at diner, which was only an hour away.

Bishop rolled the truck forward and brought it to a stop in front of the garden shed. The window the privates used to keep look out from was completely blocked, or it appeared to be by those brewers of illegal hooch.

Climbing out of the cab he walked toward the door. But before he grabbed the knob the wooden barrier swung open to prominently display Bill who wore a sardonic grin.

"Hi, Corp!" Bill said as he tried to block Bishops entry to their sanctum.

Bishop could tell that the distilling process was in full production as a wicked order reached out and took hold of his noise with the vengeance of a school master.

"Got things cooking have yea?"

"That's right Corp. But I was wondering if you could move the truck so we can keep a watch going?"

"In the jungle old friend, you don't look at the tree, but what's beyond it," Bishop instructed. "That way you can see the enemy plain as day."

"How do you mean?"

"Look through the windows of the truck. That way you have more camouflage."

Bill leaned to one side and could see the truck had been strategically parked to allow a full field of vision without being easily seen form anyone coming toward them.

"I gotcha," Bill replied as he drew himself up and stepped to one side allowing Bishop to enter.

"Okay buddy, now let's get a touch of the brill cream you got going in there," Bishop said as he poured through the door.

* * *

After dinner it was customary for the detachment to resign themselves to the pursuits of interest each man had chosen for entertainment. But before being dismissed by La Rouch he announced the next day's orders. A heads up type of informal notification for what the others could expect.

"Sergeant Wilkins," the Captain began.

"Sir."

"I noticed you've been out shopping again. Any luck?"

Everyone knew the significance of the code except Bishop. He hadn't been there long enough to learn all the little nuances of deception. Not that the chateau had been bugged by the gray mice to record conversations, but more out of habit by being vigilant in what you say out loud.

"As a matter of fact, I think we'll have a couple of sets of shorts for our Corporal in a few days."

"I'm going to need socks too," Bishop interjected. It seemed like a good time to turn in his laundry list.

"It will be waiting for you when you get back Corporal."

"When I get back sir," Bishop said in surprise. "From where?"

"Yes I'd like to know too?" Wilkins responded.

"An American plane was shot down a few days ago and the CO want's you down there to see how we do things I guess."

"By myself!"

"Hardly, you're going to join the members of Group 2."

"That will make three of them sir," Wilkins concluded.

La Rouch nodded in reply then added, "Alec will show you around."

"That's Chief Warrant Officer Alec Harper to you Corporal," Wilkins added.

"Yea Corp, bring us back some eggs eh," Ed added. "You can get'tum fresh from down there."

"How long will I be down there?"

"I'd say a week or two."

"A week or two in these clothes!"

"Don't worry Corp, will have the fumigator ready when you get back eh," Bill said as a round of laughter shot through the damp air.

"Oh man, this is gonna suck," Bishop said as he hung his head.

"Don't worry Corporal," Wilkins said. "I'll get some uniforms down to you a couple of days."

"Oh man," Bishop said in contempt.

The rest of the group was chuckling at Bishops predicament. What he didn't know was everyone went to Group 2 at one time or another for training. But this time it was beginning to feel more like retribution than information.

*　　*　　*

It was a little before midnight when the entire group was awaken by a storm of vehicle horns. Hanoi had no proper form of emergency warning devices, they were still held up in transit from Moscow. As a substitute for informing the public of a bombing mission headed their way by US B-52's, the North organized a wave of vehicle horns going off starting in the direction of the approaching aircraft and rolling over the city. And as each air raid warden sounded his horn civilians all over jumped from their beds and joined in the civil defense maneuver.

"What the hell's going on?" Bishop cried as he sprang from his room out into the hallway.

I the darkness Bishop could see Wilkins in his underwear a few feet away. By this time the entire group had rolled out and were headed downstairs to the basement to take shelter.

"Bishop!" Wilkins called out over the radiant din of the horns blearing. "Did you switch on the beacon?"

"Oh Christ, I forgot," Bishop yelled and ran toward the closet where the radio beacon equipment was.

"Judas Priest man, you're going to get us killed," Wilkins screamed as he too followed Bishop.

As Bishop flung himself into the closet he snapped the few switches on that brought up the signal. He felt the wind from the sergeants haste brush at his naked back and then turned to follow his leader.

In the attic Wilkins and Bishop ripped the canvas cover from the satellite dish and rolled it onto the dusty floor. Wilkins reached over and turned on the sending unit switch and the two stepped back making sure the equipment was operating. The tiny red power light flickered then went steady.

Then, far off in the distance the sound of bombs landing near the refinery south of the city started vibrating the building. It was the shock waves from the explosion they were feeling. Both men moved to the window and stared in the direction of pounding.

"No sweat sarg, their too far away to hit us," Bishop said making a sign of relief.

"Don't be so sure," Wilkins said. "We may be out of target range but the SRO's is what we have to worry about."

"SRO's?" Bishop asked.

"Slow Rack Ordinance," Wilkins replied. "At the altitude they drop from the hydraulics that release the bombs tends to slip and a whole rack of bombs can be strung out over miles."

"Yea, I know," Bishop answered, his throat began to go dry. "Down South we call that spread and shed."

The two men stood in the sea of conflicting noises and watched as the sky began lighting up. They waited in their own internal silence, each beginning to tremble from the anticipated anxiety. It was like watching a freight train bearing down on your position between the rails, knowing that your feet won't let you step aside.

Then, far to their right a single bomb landed in the area of the old railway bridge. A second landed a few blocks from that but closer to them. And like a giant strolling down main-street a bomb planted itself and vaporized the space around the impaction.

"Holy shit sarg, let's get the hell out of here!" Bishop screamed and the two broke from their entrancement and headed downstairs.

But before they had gone more than a few steps the shock waves hit the chateau like a tsunami. Wind and dust filled the room and knock the men to the floor. Glass from the window sailed through the air and over their heads impacting the slanted roof that formed the walls. The sound was deafening as the two scurried like rats for the stairs. Before they reached the second floor it was over.

A few more bombs landed farther on and then everything was silent like a morgue. Outside the horns had stopped and shouts for help seemed to drift away. The smell of sulfur hung in the air, and it mingled with the order of burning wood.

In the darkness Bishop and Wilkins slumped against the walls and lowered themselves to the floor across from each other.

"Are you okay?" Wilkins mumbled.

"What," Bishop replied, his ears still ringing from the blast. "Oh yea, peachy keen."

"We better check on the others and get organized."

"Yea know," Bishop said loudly. "When I see another jet jockey I'm going to by that guy the biggest drink in the bar."

Wilkins was curious. He couldn't imagine why the Corporal was not the least bit angry at being a target of his former employer.

"Why is that?" Wilkins asked.

"Because the son of a bitch missed me again."

CHAPTER 13

Bishop never liked riding in choppers, even ones with doors on them. The sound was malicious to the ears and the wind current tumbling around inside actually sucked light weight things from your pockets, like wallets and note pads. The kinds of things grunts like to keep close for identification purposes in case of tragedy.

The Hind 23 helicopter was made by the Soviets for transferring cargo and infantry to desolate locations. By the time the North got their hands on one there had been at least three newer versions. Subsequently, the older models should have been sold to the enemy instead of the Soviet's allies.

Interior lighting was nonexistent and when the bright sunshine entered the cargo area it nearly blinded the passengers to the point that instead of climbing out like normal you actually feel out the chopper. The hand hold rungs, the few there were had been placed away from the doorway so there was nothing to count on incase of accident. Coincidently, it was well known that Soviet soldiers had suffered more casualties getting out, than being shot at.

The ride down to Bong Loc took a little over three hours and Bishop, due to the terrible vibrations caused by the main rotor, felt like he had been riding in a box car from Chicago to Miami.

When they landed at the small airstrip used mostly by rotary aircraft, Bishop was amazed at what he saw. It felt like he was back down South around Hue or Phu Bai. The airstrip was inside a huge fire support base complete with PSP runways and sandbagged bunkers and wooden hooch's.

Bishop couldn't imagine the North having the same kind of design for their bases as the Americans. But when he thought about it, why not? American fire bases had hardly ever been overrun on a one to one basis. It usually was at least twenty to one in favor of the North to take a complex. At least that's what he remembered when he was at Khe Sanh during Tet of 1968.

Once out of the rotor-wash and the mist that swirled around in it, Bishop made his way over to a small hut looking much like a porcupine hunched over a log. It was bristling with antennas and he concluded it was the air traffic control tower.

"I need a ride!" Bishop called to the round oriental face on the other side of a small window.

The face kept starring back at him in confusion without any sign of vocal response.

"Corporal Bishop!" a voice called from behind him.

Bishop tuned to see a Private Second walking towards him through the whirling mist. It was obvious by the man's gate that he had spent a great deal of time outdoors and the weather had no effect on him. And Bishop knew firsthand what that was like.

"You my ride," Bishop asked as the man was within arm's length.

"You got it eh!" the young man said.

Bishop guessed the young soldier was in his early twenties because the war hadn't set into his facial features yet. That was one thing Bishop had learned, in combat age was determined by time in the field, and not by the number of years.

"My shit's in with the rest on the chopper."

The young man paused with a curious look in his expression.

"They made you carp on the floor Corporal?"

"No man, my stuff, my kit, my duffle bag!"

"Oh sorry eh," the man replied with a chuckle. "You're the yank, that's why I didn't get it."

"Yea right," Bishop said as he led his driver to the helicopter that had just now shut down its engine. The blades kept rotating and made little sound.

The two men grabbed the few things Bishop had brought with him, including his dress green uniform. Not that he was expecting to turn out for parade, but that at least he would have something to wear while waiting for what Wilkins was going to send him.

The vehicle the Private was driving was formerly a Soviet built three quarter ton Jeep. The type used by command officers to cruise around Moscow in. Subsequently, it was design for paved roads not tank trails which made the ride less than enjoyable.

The vehicle was in the Soviet Army green paint scheme and the letters UN painted in white were on the hood instead of the side. Not bad if you were being observed from the air, but from the side you were just another RPG magnet.

"Okay private, you know my name what's yours?"

"Oh Right," he said. "The names Tommy Summers Corp," extending his hand.

The two followed the traditional greeting of gentlemen and then climbed into the Jeep. The engine popped into submission and they made for the highway.

CHAPTER 14

The ride through the North's base was very informative for Bishop who, never thought after chasing them around in the jungle, caves, and tunnels, they could ever have something like this. Barber shops, uniform cleaning, clubs and even a theater were open to view. They even had a firehouse complete with 1940's fire trucks. Unfortunately they were made by Renault which explained why most buildings were burnt to the ground before they got there.

The main road that trekked the entire length of Vietnam was Highway One. It stayed on the sea side part of the country and its off shoots went deeper into jungle and mountain terrain. Its only break was at the Demilitarized Zone which was on the 17th parallel, or close to it. Bishop was about eight miles north of the DMZ and for the most part traffic was made up of bicycles and small trucks. Cars were nearly nonexistent and driving along it was common to run into huge clusters of pedestrian foot traffic carrying their wears on their backs to market.

This was the central part of Vietnam and Bishop was used to seeing the same sights down in the South. The road stretched out like a long gray ribbon between miles of surrounding rice paddies. Each paddy was about two acres in size and was subdivide by foot dikes, small raised earth works that the farmers used as trails to the work site.

From the air it looked like a greenish patchwork quilt and scattered along were small hamlets secluded in collections of tall trees. In a broader view, the villages looked more like islands set on a gray rope.

"So where the hell is this fast mover supposed to be down at," Bishop asked.

The Corporal's right foot rested on the door frame of the jeep as he slumped comfortably in the seat.

56

Tommy glanced over at the new arrival not sure if he should hand out information to someone he didn't know. Especially when he's dressed in the same uniform.

"Fast mover?" Tommy queried. It was the first time he had heard the term applied to a jet fighter.

"Yea fox four, jet fighter, you know the type." Bishop was becoming annoyed with Tommy's lack of common phraseology.

Clearing his throat Tommy replied. "It's just south of the next village."

"How far out is it from the road?"

"Not far, you'll see it when we go by eh."

Bishop nodded and went back to observing the countryside. A habit he was familiar with in case of ambush. He wanted to know which way to run when the shit hit the fan.

They crossed the open landscape in good time and passed through the small village they were approaching. Nothing looked out of the ordinary to Bishop. This was a good sign.

People wondered around the village dressed in bright colored attire, typical of the peasant population. Pigs and goats tugged at their tethers as dogs barked out the warning of momentary strangers to the small community.

Once through Tommy picked up the pace on the open road as Bishop scanned the tree line for any signs of the crashed plane. Seeing nothing he asked, "Where did you say that bird was?"

"Just around the bend and down about a mile," Tommy said not taking his eyes off the road ahead.

As they made the described turn Bishop could see the landscape spread out like a huge valley. The road ran straight into another small town surrounded by trees and it looked a lot like the one they had just passed through. Far to his right he could see the tree line that usually was a land mark for the jungles edge.

Just as they were about to enter the village, Bishop spotted it. Lying on its side with just a small part of the wing sticking up out of the paddy was the green camouflaged fighter. It was difficult to see with the backdrop of the jungles edge, but the shadowed silhouette was unmistakable.

"Pull over Tommy!"

"We're not supposed to stop on the road Corp."

"I don't give a shit, stop the truck."

"Okay, but the boss ain't going to like eh."

Tommy brought the jeep to a halt within fifty feet of the village boundary. Smoke from the cooking fires inside the hooch's hung like a blanket in the damp air. A light breeze from the coast a few miles away made the palm trees quiver like dogs shaking off the bath water.

"Common Tommy lets go."

"Judas Priest Corp they'll skin us a live if we get out of the truck."

"Never mind, let's go!" Bishop ordered and the two climbed from the safety of their vehicle into the gathering storm which was certain to follow.

The two Canadian's with Bishop in the lead made their way along the road and entered the village where the closest paddy met the island community. A fenced walkway paralleled the border and as they walked briskly along peasants started emerging from their houses. Gradually being surrounded by a tempest of chatter unlike a protest rally in Washington, the two were pursued by the ever growing mob.

"Corp, where the hell you going eh?"

"To check out that plane. I was sent down here to do that."

The two were talking to each other like men on patrol. The faster they walked the louder they talked.

"But Corp we're not allowed out there."

"So how do you know it's ours and not theirs?"

"WE don't!" Tommy said as he came to a halt and instantly was immersed in a sea of chattering peasants.

Bishop kept walking. He was aware of the basic layout of the village and knew that there had to be a main dike that went out in the direction of the plane. It was merely a matter of finding it before he too would be blocked by the angry population.

Now in a full jog Bishop slipped past houses and over small fences to end up where he wanted to be. Standing there at the edge of the long dike he could see the planes location. But just as he was about to head out a voice called to him above the din of the oncoming crowd.

"You STOP. You Stop!"

Bishop turned to see a unformed soldier heading towards him leading the pack. Not far behind he could see Tommy's head bobbing above the crowd.

In that clouded moment of uncertainty Bishop took the initiative and headed out onto the dike. Only going a few feet he stopped. Looking down at the dike he could see foot prints in the mud holding puddles of water in them. It hadn't been long he deduced that people had been along the trail, but which people and how many?

"You stop, no go there," the soldier screamed.

Bishop turned as if captured by the soldiers words and retraced his steps.

"You not go out there," the soldier said firmly. "Land mines."

Bishop stood before the soldier and noticed the rank badge. The soldier was a sergeant in the Regional Police Force, known as the gray mice, out of town type.

The sergeant was dressed in a gray tunic with a couple of medals pinned to it and he was wearing a green pith helmet with the red star glaringly centered. His pants were recently pressed and lacked the usual shine produced by inactivity.

"Who the hell are you?" Bishop asked.

"Sergeant Trang, RPF."

Bishop looked down at the sergeant's right wrist and spotted a watch that seemed to be the size of a trash can lid. It had all the bells and whistles common to cheap watches sold in Saigon.

"So what dead American did you rip that off of?" Bishop said as he reached down and hoisted Trang's wrist into the air like a trophy.

Trang's eyes widened. He had never met a Canadian with such contempt and arrogance. It was baffling and insulting at the same time and the sergeant didn't know what to say. What was even more problematic was the Canadian sounded more like the Americans he knew when he roamed the cities down south as a former South Vietnamese soldier.

"You say there are land mines out there?" Bishop said pointing in the direction of the dike. "I say bull shit."

"No bull shit, mines," Trang said firmly as he trounced his confusion and became more aggressive, more typical of his position.

"Yea right," Bishop replied as he broke through the crowd and stormed toward a nearby hooch.

Glancing through the open door the Corporal recognized an ejection seat from a jet leaning against the plaster wall. On a small shelf was a clock from the instrument panel wired to a nine volt Eveready battery. They both looked in good condition and were a recent acquisition.

Bishop turned his attention to what he really wanted, a barking dog tied to a stake beside the door.

"You look like you could use some exercise boy," Bishop said as he untied the leash which was about a twenty foot length of rope.

"Christ Corp you're going to get use killed." Tommy replied as he shoved his way through the crowd and met Bishop by the dike.

"You listen to Private he know," Trang called as he tried to block Bishop's approach.

"How do you know he's a private?"

"He private you corporal, you know better. You take order I Sergeant Trang RFP!"

"Stay behind me Tommy about ten feet."

"Corp, he says there are mines out there."

"There aren't any mines. Look at the rice, they just cut it a day or two ago," Bishop said with contempt. "Come on mutt, let's take a hike," Bishop added as he twirled around to get the rope free form his body.

The dog had woven himself to Bishop as the crowd lowered their collective voices and watched.

Like a blind man being led by his seeing-eye dog the two walked forward along the dike. Bishop was all too aware of how useful dogs were at sniffing out explosives. The smell of cordite was like a shot from a cannon to the canine.

With Tommy close behind the two man patrol wondered out onto the dike. The farther out they went the quieter it got. Bishop concluded it was nearly a quarter mile out to the crash site and the dog seemed to be in a panic to get there. Bishop thought it was the promise of a free lunch from the jungle that kept the dog prodding onward.

At the three quarter mark Bishop stopped and dropped to his knees, an instinctual action. Never approach a tree line standing up unless you know it's safe. But he was unsure as to what might be near the plane which was clearly visible in the paddy.

With the dog tugging at the rope and beginning to bark like a hound after pheasant, Bishop rose and walked slowly ahead. His eyes were trained on the muddy path that now had bare foot steps and boot prints mingled together. It became obvious that not only were the peasants out here but so were many soldiers.

"Okay Tommy, you got a note pad and pen handy?"

"Right Corp," Tommy replied as the two were now directly across from the wreckage.

"Here, take the mutt," Bishop said handing over the leash. Then feeling with his boot he slid down the embankment until he was knee deep in the cold water.

"Watch it Corp they might have mines in there."

"No sweat, they wouldn't trap it on this side, but the side closest to the jungle."

"Why?"

"In case the pilot comes back and tries to grab some gear."

Bishop eased through the paddy making little waves as he went. The wreckage was about a hundred feet out and he could see the raked dirt the craft plowed up as it landed.

The jet was a Navy type F-6 Convair. Camouflage paint was on the top while a white belly lay half submerged in the water. The edges of the delta wings had little damage which meant the pilot had landed it without rolling it over.

As Bishop inched closer he spotted the large holes in the side made by anti-aircraft fire which also meant the pilot was flying low at tree top level.

He paused just short of the tail section and looked back toward the village. There was no sign of anyone coming out after them and at the same time he spotted a large built up area a little farther south of the village. It was obviously the source of the shell holes.

"Hey Tommy, write this down," Bishop called, and then relayed the numbers off the stabilizer which was under water.

Bishop moved ahead and climbed up onto the wing making his way to the cockpit. Straddling the Plexiglas he looked down and noticed all the gages were gone including the ejection seat. He noticed there were know burn marks caused when the seat is fired out of the plane with the pilot in it. This meant the pilot was loose somewhere and the locals had disassembled the seat to take it out.

Reaching down Bishop wiped moisture from the small tag listing the aircraft official number and called out the digits to Tommy who quickly recorded them. He then leaned over the right side and spotted the name of the pilot and crew chief. This was a common practice for air crews so they could identify the plane later. The name of the pilot was Ensign JG Tony Blake, crew chief Martin Harrington.

After calling out the names Bishop slid down the side of the fuselage into the paddy water. He inspected the empty bomb racks and noticed they were rusted. This meant the plane wasn't on a bombing mission. He concluded rightly the plane was probably on a low level reconnaissance flight.

As he turned to head back to the dike Bishop heard a sploosh behind him. It was the sound of something small dropping into the water. Turning back he surveyed the bottom of the paddy. The water rippled the view but a shiny object caught his eye. It was a small caliber pistol bullet.

Bishop slowly raised his head and scanned the jungle tree line not more than fifty feet away. The green of the drab foliage was like looking into a unfocused kaleidoscope, but he had learned to not look at what was in front, but just behind. It was then that he spotted it.

"Oh shit," Bishop whispered.

CHAPTER 15

There was a time when Sergeant Wilkins had played with the notion of taking up the sport of golf. Not in a professional manner, but just enough to whip the officers out of their meager wagers. And while standing on the corner across the street from the Krakow Club at Tri Bang and Do Ho streets he thought of how wonderful it had been if the North had made the former city dump a golf course rather than a decaying monument to a former communist. A Communist by the way, that did little to make their lives better.

This was evident by the lack of communication between people in the city. For the most part, the decaying old French installed phone lines hung like rotting rope from the polls. The polls themselves leaned precariously because the soil they had been planted in couldn't stand the weight. So when Wilkins checked the telex machine after dropping Bishop off at the airport, he read the coded message informing him that his laundry was ready. The telex was the only communication device between Group 6 and the Canadian embassy.

The message was sent by a private in the supply room at the embassy and the underling had no compunction to think the words stood for anything else than what was clearly stated. What the private didn't know was that the message began in the Polish embassy across town and had been called in by Sergeant Pogozinski. His foreign accent was hard enough to understand and sounded just as confusing as the Vietnamese pigeon English.

Dressed in his subversive uniform which looked like a Polish paratrooper, Wilkins crossed the broad avenue and entered the hangout of the Polish contingent. As usual, Pogozinski and his band of brothers occupied the long table and full glasses of beer were spotted in front of each member.

A second chorus of a polish paratrooper song was in full swing when Wilkins joined the Warsaw Pack leader. In a single motion Pogozinski took Wilkins by the arm and led him to a small table in the corner. A porthole of a window looked out over the intersection and would provide plenty of warning incase the unfriendly Soviets showed up.

"You boys sure know how to drink eh?" Wilkins commented, the others slamming down their drinks as if in a race to reach inebriation before diner.

"You got better things to do?"

"Not at the moment."

"Good, then you join us yes?"

"Not just yet, I'm still on duty."

"Okay, I got your uniforms in my car. It's around corner in trunk."

"The trunk locked?"

"No, just wiggle handle."

"Thanks Pogo. I know someone who's going to appreciate this."

"Yes, I save Polish government lots of money today," the sergeant said as he shifted his weight in the chair. "Now I got something else for you."

"The printing press?" Wilkins asked eagerly.

Once Captain La Rouch took Wilkins into his confidence about the MPC counterfeit money, the sergeant began to think of another route to discover the truth.

The Captain was looking for the stacks of money which were being shifted around by the North so to not be discovered. This meant that trucks would have to be used and the money housed someplace safe. This also meant a lot of probing that usually ended up for nothing and could upset the wrong people.

Wilkins on the other hand took his self-proclaimed mission as to finding the printing press. If that was discovered the money couldn't be too far away. It also meant that moving a printing press and all the paraphernalia that was attached to the process would be easier to discover.

"I did police check with Warsaw, they say type you need would be made by Check's. They technical type you know?"

"I know. The Americans have been watching them for years."

"They also say that press would have to be in always dry place. Plates could rust in rain. Paper ink if wet all bad."

"Of course. Now all I have to do is find a dry warehouse somewhere in the city."

"You kid! Even roof in embassy leak like old boot."

Wilkins grinned at the comment but the Pol was right. Finding a dry place during pre–monsoon in Hanoi would be almost impossible. Nearly every roof in the city had a dozen shrapnel holes in it.

"Thanks Pogo, send me a bill on this one."

The two men rose from their seats and shook hands. But the Pol didn't let go right away.

"I got problem too you know."

Wilkins was impatient but he knew listening to his counterpart wouldn't take long and probably wouldn't amount to much.

"So what's your problem eh?"

"Okay," Pogo began. "Our government. State agriculture. Want to sell combines here in this country."

"Sorry my friend I don't have anything to do with that."

"Yes I know," Pogo replied as he swung an arm over Wilkins shoulder drawing him near.

"Canada want same thing yes?"

"That's the rumor."

"My Minister want to convince North to buy superior product from us."

"You got to be kidding. Capitalists make the best combines in the world," Wilkins boasted.

"I know, since Russians take over factory they make nothing but junk. They gave my father a combine and three months later he strip off thrasher and build a cabin on back. Now it school bus."

Wilkins grinned again as the image of such a contraption maneuvering through the school yard came to mind.

"What Minister want is recommendation by your embassy to watch test in two months."

Wilkins leaned back taken by surprise by the request that couldn't possibly be arranged. He couldn't get a travel pass approved in two months much less a referral.

"Pogo, that's way beyond me."

"No, all we need is embassy paper with symbol on top. That all."

"Who's going to write up the referral?"

"Moscow probably," Pogo said sadly. "They put name of old embassy governor on it and by the time it checked the demonstration over."

"Judas Priest, if they ever found out I'd be sent to Siberia."

"You not worry. Pogo take care of friends."

Wilkins stepped out of the bear hug the Pol had him in. He paused and starred at the floor wondering how he could do the deed. Then, looking up he said firmly," I'll have it for you in a few days."

Pogo smiled and went back to join his comrades.

Wilkins made for the door and the Polish staff car with the uniforms in the trunk. When all was considered, the Canadian's were still up one nothing.

CHAPTER 16

It was amazing how dumb dogs can be. There the mutt sat beside Tommy like they had just stopped to rest on their Sunday outing. The bulk of the rope Tommy held as a leash was lying coiled in the mud, and all the mutt could do is raise its leg and lick himself.

"Did you find something Corp?" Tommy called out.

"I think I gotta go," Bishop called back. "You stay there don't move."

"Heck of time for a bowel movement eh!"

"Can't be helped. Stay there I said!"

With that Bishop slowly moved toward the tree line and the man just inside it. Glancing over his should he could see that the crashed plane was between him and the village which meant no one could see what he was up to.

Reaching the bank Bishop stepped from the paddy up onto a path that circled the entire area and hugged the tree line. The bush in front of him shuttered as the man slipped back farther into the jungle. Keeping low, Bishop traced the steps of the stranger, whom he was about to meet.

"Boy am I glad to see you," the stranger said stopping in a small clearing.

"Well, I'm not glad to see you sir," Bishop replied as the two shook hands.

Bishop could see the nervousness of the man who wore the gray flight suite of an Air Force pilot. The black leather tag over his right pocket read, Captain Benjamin Cook, USAF. Over his shoulder the officer wore a holster with a 38 caliber pistol in it.

Of medium build, Cook had dark eyes that seemed to appear as if he had been starring into the sun too long.

"You're with the UN aren't you," Cook said. Then leaning slightly to get a look at the two stripes on the sleeve added, "Corporal?"

"Yes sir, names Bishop I'm with the Canadian contingent."

"What luck soldier. You were heaven sent," Cook said with a sign of relief.

The Captain was told that if he ever was shot down to try for a UN camp. But in North Vietnam he'd have better luck trying to swim to Hawaii.

"All I can say is," Bishop began. "Somebody up there has to have a real good sense of humor."

"You got to get me out of here. Give me diplomatic immunity or something."

"Hold on a second sir," Bishop said trying to calm the man down a bit. "Is that your bird out there?"

"Yes, of course."

"Then what the hell is an air force captain doing flying a navy fox four?"

Cook suddenly stopped being nervous and went on the defensive. "That's none of your business Corporal."

"I'm making it my business sir. Those damn dinks are going to shoot me between the eyes if they catch me and I want to have a good story."

"Exactly Corporal. It's a good story."

"What the fuck do mean sir?"

Cook said nothing and starred at Bishop in a manner that made the Corporal begin to fear his new acquisition.

It then started to sink in for Bishop. The only reason an air force pilot would be flying a navy jet was to conceal the mission he was on. If captured the conflicting evidence, navy air force, would keep the interrogators guessing. Perhaps long enough for Cook to make his escape.

"Damn sir," Bishop said as he took a step backward. "You were on a one way trip?"

"Something like that. Now you see why I need your help?"

"But there weren't any bombs on the racks. Did you dump them off somewhere?"

"No Corporal. I was making a delivery."

"Oh shit!"

Bishop himself had never witnessed a special drop which usually meant something sinister was about to end up to close for comfort.

Typically a special drop wasn't an explosive device but something to do with either reconnaissance or support of technical equipment. The air force would send in a fast moving jet to get by antiaircraft defenses and then drop the package near the intended target, which was usually some infiltrator. The Green Berets were usually the infiltrators.

Something was odd about the Corporal, Cook thought. He sounded too much like a lost American than a Canadian. The uniform Bishop wore looked right, but it was more of an instinctual question. The kind that happens when you discover the man you're playing poker with has got one too many cards in his hand.

"So what are you going to do?" Cook asked.

"I don't know sir."

"You're going to protect me right?"

"Christ sir, we can't even protect ourselves. And on top of that I just got here."

"That man you were calling to. Who is he?"

"Ah. Tommy something. He's my ride to the base."

"What base?"

"It's Group 2. We're here to report belligerent infractions and collect evidence. In fact I'm supposed to bring back a piece of your plane for proof."

"Back to where exactly?"

"The Canadian embassy in Hanoi."

"That's not the direction I want to go in."

"No shit sir," Bishop replied as he turned slightly. His internal clock for taking a dump was expiring.

As if cued in, Tommy called out from the dike, "He Corp, you just about done. There's someone headed this way."

"Now what?" Cook asked in disgust.

"I ain't got a fuck'en clue sir. But have you got a place to hide?"

"Yea, there's a cave over by the creek."

"Okay, dig in and eat what the monkeys eat. I'll try to get back to you."

"Hey Corp, hustle your bustle!"

"Okay Tommy, I'm comin!" and with that Bishop turned and hastily slipped back to the side of the jet.

Snatching up a piece of broken rudder control flap with the aircrafts number on it, Bishop made for the side of the dike and the barking dog that now seemed to know who the real enemy was.

CHAPTER 17

The small group of four North Vietnamese soldiers reached the place where Tommy and the dog were. At about the same time Bishop was pulling himself out of the paddy water. The dog made growling noises but stayed behind Tommy's legs.

Handing the piece of stabilizer to his partner Bishop turned to face the four belligerents.

"Told ya Corp," Tommy said as he accepted the piece of aircraft debris.

"Never mind I'll take care of this."

"You bet eh?"

As if on parade Bishop drew himself up to attention, straightened his blue beret and prepared for the worst. He knew when addressing officers it's best to show them some form of respect. Even if he didn't mean it.

"I'm Captain Tri Hoc," the closest soldier said facing Bishop.

"Yes Captain," Bishop replied as he snapped a salute.

The officer responded with the customary acknowledgement.

"What are you doing here Corporal?" the captain asked noticing Bishops sleeve rank.

"I'm with the UN observation group I was sent here to get information on this plane you shot down."

"I did not shoot the plane down. You must be mistaken."

"I didn't mean you personally sir."

"I know what you meant," Hoc replied with a slight grin. He was testing Bishops savvy because he had encountered the Canadian's lack of being able to think quickly before. His opinion of the leadership at Group 2 was unfaltering.

"May I see your travel pass?"

"Ahhh Tommy. Have we got one?"

"Yea somewhere Corp." Tommy replied. "I think it's back in the Jeep eh?"

"I'll get it for you sir."

"Not necessary, I know what it says and it does not allow you to go any further than three meters off the road."

"It does," Bishop said with surprise. "I didn't know that sir. You see I just arrived."

"That's understandable," Hoc said with a grin. "But your driver should know it."

Bishop glanced around at Tommy who was almost as nervous as the dog.

"Well, he was just following my orders sir."

"That is understandable too, but you are both under arrest."

"For what?"

"Trespassing," Hoc replied as he signaled his sergeant to handcuff the two.

"You can't cuff him," Bishop protested as he was first to be restrained.

"Why not?"

"Who's going to drive our truck?"

"My sergeant will drive. Not to worry he good driver."

"Does your sergeant have a Canadian driver's license?"

"He doesn't need one. We are not in Canada."

"You will be if you sit in that jeep."

Hoc smiled and then turned to one of the other officers. Stepping back so they would not be over heard they conversed for what seemed like an eternity. With heads nodding, Hoc stepped back in front of Bishop.

"Okay, you come with us. He go to camp."

In a diplomatic situation it was nearly impossible to tell a bluff from a threat, and the North was good at erroring on the side of neutrality.

As Bishop was escorted away with the sergeant holding him by the shoulder he called out to Tommy. "Get back and tell them what's happed!"

"Right Corp!" Tommy called from a safe trailing distance. The dog sniffing at his heals.

"You know where I'll be!"

"Right Corp," Tommy called. "I told ya eh?"

CHAPTER 18

Captain La Rouch was seated at his desk in the small room he called home at Group 6. The light of day was fading quickly because of the season. Pre-monsoon kept everything in a faded glow that seemed to even get under the bed sheets before it should. Between his long fingers he was twirling the small MPC currency note as if it was going to tell him where it was from.

He heard a horn sound in the driveway and wondered who it was. Crossing over to the door to his room the Captain opened it and looked into the entry room beyond. With no clue as to who honked, La Rouch strolled to the main door which was slightly ajar. Peering out he spotted Bill in the seat of their pickup truck, the vehicle was pointing outbound.

"Hey Bill, "La Rouch called as he opened the door fully.

"Yes sir!"

"Where are you going this time of day?"

"Out to the airport sir. Our supplies just came in."

"What Noooow?"

"Yes sir, we got a message from ops, the plane was late due to weather."

"Hold on, I'm going with you," The Captain called back and went to his room to retrieve his beret and travel pass. He was sure to need it at this late hour.

Climbing into the blue truck, La Rouch and Bill road through the busy streets. It was rush hour and bicycle traffic was heavier than normal due to the incoming meteorological conditions.

When the winds picked up at this time of year it usually meant a long rain lasting several days. A precursor of the severity of the storms had kept planes grounded for most of the day, and the temporary reprieve allowed the last Air

Canada plane to touch down. Then like a dragon closing its mouth, the weather turned sour again.

When they arrived at the airport they drove straight through onto the tarmac where the plane was parked, doors open waiting for delivery.

There was no sentry at the small shack at the main gate because so little air traffic didn't warrant the security measure. In fact, having a guard was a nuisance because nobody wanted to get wet having to wake the man up every half hour.

"You get started unloading and I'll check in," La Rouch commanded.

Bill slowed the truck down enough for the Captain to drop off and trot into the terminal building. The wind tugged at his uniform and beret as if to warn him of something yet unseen.

La Rouch made his way inside and found the desk where Lieutenant Ho Buc usually parked himself. The desk was an old accounts roll up desk, but it had seen better years. The top of the desk was high enough to act as a counter where everyone checked in.

The echoing sound of La Rouch closing the outside door had given Buc a chance to hide what he was writing in one of the top drawers. It was a personal correspondence.

"You late tonight?" Buc said as La Rouch loomed up behind the makeshift counter.

"Yes, weather you know?"

"Yes, got travel pass?"

"Yes, right here," La Rouch said as he pulled the document from his upper pocket.

It was necessary for there to be a validation stamp on the pass. If stopped by the gray mice without it, La Rouch and Bill would be headed for the guard house.

Buc slid open a drawer and taking the pass opened it to the first page. It had several lines drawn diagonally where the stamp was to be placed. Without a word Buc stamped the pass and handed it back to the smiling Captain. La Rouch was making a gesture of thanks without specifically stating it.

La Rouch tucked the travel pass back inside his pocket and glanced over the desk top. More as a curious nature considering he didn't speak or read the local dialect. A few forms were resting on the corner but that was all of note.

Turning the Captain walked casually back to the only window open to the outside. There was a posting board next to it and next to that was a small magazine rack. La Rouch scanned the different publications all of varying thicknesses and each had some kind of cover art designed to attract readers, especially those in Moscow and Hungary.

Randomly selecting one of the magazines with a picture of a very alluring woman scantily clad holding a bottle of Vodka, La Rouch thumbed through the glossy pages. With everything written in Russian, La Rouch was batting zero for information gathering. But the pictures held a considerable interest.

Being certain his mother wouldn't approve of the subject matter, La Rouch replaced the mag amongst a horde of others. Then as if he was employed as a distributor's assistant, he straightened the collection to make it appear more proper.

When he was finished he glanced over at Lieutenant Buc and noticed he was bent over writing. Thinking he might garner something of interest in his visit the Captain casually walked back to the desk and leaned against the top as if to order a meal.

"You need help?" Buc asked.

La Rouch paused contemplating the suggestion. Did the Lieutenant mean in a psychiatric, physical, or possibly even metaphysical manner?

Not completely sure the Captain asked, "What are you writing?"

Buc was suddenly taken back. It was as if he was being scrutinized by the enemy.

"I write letter to wife and family," Buc replied with just enough contempt to aggravate most people to not ask any more questions. But La Rouch wasn't just anyone.

"Doesn't your family live around here?"

"No," Buc replied. He leaned back in his chair and held the pen like a chopstick.

"They live in South."

It was then La Rouch glanced over at the half opened drawer nearest Buc's arm. In side were many envelopes tied together with some string. He couldn't discern how many where there, but it appeared obvious they weren't intended to be mailed.

"Are all those letters too?" La Rouch said pointing to the half open drawer.

"Yes. I write one a week."

"Why don't you mail them?"

"No can do. Mail can't go south out of this country."

La Rouch stepped back from the counter and rubbed his cleanly shaved chin. He wasn't old enough for a five o'clock shadow, but the act broke his concentration enough for him to think things through.

Buc could help with his mission to locate the phony currency, if it was brought through the airport from some other country. Even if it didn't provide any proof to his argument, a bit of kindness could go a long way in other areas of interest. Like not having new comers to the unit interrogated or held up for no real reason.

"Look it," La Rouch began. "I think I can get them to your family for you."

"How you do that?" Buc replied with considerable interest.

"We have a diplomatic pouch that goes down to Saigon every day. I could put the letters in there and have them mailed from the embassy to the address."

Buc wasn't a real smart man but he knew an opportunity when he saw one, and this had to be a whopper. He could at last be in touch with his distant family whom he loved and admired. Before coming North he and his father were very highly placed in the local import export company that brought US goods to Saigon. Everything from soap to sun glasses where among the products that did well in the economy. Even wrist watches.

"What you want for this?"

"Nothing."

Buc turned away to appear as if he was thinking it through.

"Well there is something."

"I think so. No free lunch right?"

La Rouch grinned at the truism. The American influence was everywhere and Communism was going to have a heck of time getting it sorted out.

"It's like this you see," La Rouch began. "I need to know if any large shipments of air freight come into this country from outside Vietnam."

"What kind large shipments?"

"You know. A large box or suite cases with guards around them."

"Guards?"

"Yes, something that needs a lot of security."

"Even from Canada?"

"No not from Canada, just the other counties that fly in here."

"You looking for something."

"Yes, but I don't know what it is eh?"

"Must be important if have guards?"

"I would think so."

"Not have anything like that come here. Just tourist and soldiers come here."

"Yes, I guessed that much. I just want you to let me know if you see something like that come in here."

Buc leaned forward with his head hung down. The exchange seemed more in his favor than the Canadians, and he didn't know what exactly they were looking for. So to keep his mail box open he decided he could make things up. It would at least look like he was complying with his part of the agreement.

Reaching inside the drawer Buc retrieved the letters and laid them on the counter. He then got up out of his chair and walked over to the magazine rack and took out one of the publications and started sifting through it.

La Rouch, new to the world of subversion kept his eyes on Buc. The Captain paused as if not knowing witch way to turn. He then slid the letters off the counter holding them under his arm like a football and made for the door.

Outside, La Rouch could see Bill closing up the tailgate of their truck. The wind had picked up even more than before and he walked like a man carrying a great load on his back.

Undaunted, the Captain reached the vehicle and both men drove back to Group 6.

*   *   *

From the second floor offices of the terminal building, most of which were vacant and in real need of repair, Colonel Chin stood watching the incoming storm. The Breath of the Dragon, which is what the Chinese called it, was fast approaching from the northwest and it smelt like dried fish.

Chin's field of vision included the tarmac and those scurrying around on it. The Colonel would have had to been blind to not see the Canadian officer, holding something in is arm, forcing his way through the gusts of wind to the blue pickup.

Not a common sight, Chin thought. A foreign national carrying something that looked like a small package from the customs office. They never got anything that came in small bundles to be given to anyone. If ever, it would be handled through the individual consulates.

"I must talk to Lieutenant Buc," Chin muttered. "Nobody is supposed to get free gifts."

CHAPTER 19

If it were the first time Bishop had been held in captivity, he might have started worrying about his fate shortly after being physically tossed into his cell. Experience has shown that if you look more crazy than those who share your new domicile with, then chances of survival become very good.

The first thing he did was to take off all his clothes and sit naked in the middle of the cell. This obviously got the attention of the guards and when they came to rescue his inmates, Bishop's added touch of biting the first uniform to lay hands on him was enough to get a smack across the face. And as was anticipated, Bishop was rushed off and locked in a cell the size of a high school gym locker. This might not have been so bad had they given him his clothes back, but that option didn't apply.

The overnight stay was racked occasional by someone screaming don't kill me in Vietnamese. Bishop thought this to be a strange request when he considered the screamer didn't have much choice. But it did indicate to the interrogators they were getting close to the answers they wanted.

The morning breakfast bell sounded more like a hammer tenderizing a steel can. The sound seemed to last forever and it suddenly occurred to Bishop that if it took that much coaxing to get people out of bed, then wouldn't it be better to just let them die in peace? One of the attributes of communism is that you can't die until the paperwork is finished. How terribly efficient the commies are.

The first sign of natural light met Bishops reddened eyes at around ten that morning. His locker door was swung open to the sound of rusted hinges which he missed when he was first deposited inside. They slammed the door so fast the hinges didn't have much to complain about.

Assisted by two guards Bishop was hustled down a narrow hall into the Commandants office. The room was well kept and Captain Tri Hoc was comfortably slouched in his chair. On the wall behind him was the North Vietnamese flag, the red star in the center surrounded the captains head like a halo.

"You seem to be out of uniform Corporal," Major Tennyson pointed out appropriately.

Bishop, who was making an attempt to conceal the more delicate parts of his naked body, glanced over his shoulder in the direction of the voice. He recognized Tennyson as being a Major in the Canadian Forces and that was about all. He then turned his eyes forward and spotted Captain Tri Hoc's face. The man was grinning at something which made Bishop extremely uncomfortable.

"Yes sir, I am."

"Then we should find you a uniform and have you put it on."

"Yes sir."

With a wave of his hand Hoc signaled one of his men to take Bishop to the interrogation room where he would have his uniform returned to him.

"The Canadian government is deeply sorry for the inconvenience Corporal Bishop has caused you. And we hope you will accept our apology?"

"Yes major," Hoc said as he rose from his chair. "Our government also wishes to express its willingness to help Canadians to get facts."

The minor infraction would be handled farther up the diplomatic chain and any unwarranted reprisals would merely exacerbate the issues. The fact that the embassy Adjutant had made a special trip down to the area by helicopter indicated Bishops troubles would not be over for some time.

The two officers shock hands as gentlemen sometimes do and Tennyson returned to the same jeep Bishop was in the day before. He took his place in the passenger side and waited for his driver, Bishop to join him. They would be alone for the ride to Group 2's basecamp.

The wind had picked up in the short time Tennyson had arranged Bishops release. Most of it was just paperwork and his presence was more ceremonial than official. But it was necessary just the same.

"Sorry about that sir," Bishop said as he slid into the driver's seat and switched on the motor.

"Drive on Corporal," Tennyson ordered firmly.

Without hesitation Bishop back the vehicle out onto the empty main road and swung around heading south.

Shortly leaving the village they drove past what looked like a small firebase on their right, complete with anti-aircraft battery. Bishop recognized it as the one that shot down Captain Cook's plane.

Bishop was constantly glancing at the base and was memorizing as many details as he could. It was a landmark that might prove important later on. At one point he almost drove off the road, but caught himself before tragedy struck.

Once passed the installation Tennyson order his driver to pull over on a wide shoulder used to avoid large trucks by the locals.

Bishop complied and pulled the jeep over on the deserted road. He put the shifting knob in neutral and sat rigidly in his seat. He knew he was about to be flayed for his actions, and this was probably going to be the warm up.

"You know Corporal," Tennyson began as he made himself more comfortable. "If I had you with me in Cypress I think we might have gotten a better shake for the natives."

"Well," Bishop replied, then thinking for a moment of the meaning of the comment he added," thank you sir."

"You see, you're a warrior and a dam good one," Tennyson went on almost philosophically. "I've seen your record. But the reason why the Canadian Army doesn't keep warriors around is they get things done and cause a hell of a lot of trouble doing it. The kind of trouble we're not in the business of."

"Yes sir."

"I know you were doing what you were sent down here to do. But there are protocols that have to followed, or we'll be tossed out on our ears. That would be a bloody shame if you get my meaning."

"Yes sir."

"So don't rock the boat. There's a lot you don't know and a lot of people are doing fine work here, us included. If the North ever gets wind of it we could be in serious trouble. Not only militarily, but politically and even economically as well. We send a lot of aid to this country and that keeps jobs at home. Do you understand?

"Yes sir."

"Good, you've been warned. Now let's go."

"Ah sir, now that we can chat openly, can I ask a question?"

"Make it short."

"Okay, you know that plane out there?"

"Yes what about it?"

"What are we going to do about the pilot?"

"What pilot?"

"The man flying the plane sir. He's still out there."

"Why hasn't he tried to escape?"

In his typical sarcastic manner Bishop replied, "I don't know sir. He's probably waiting for a bus."

"He's been out there a week or more," Tennyson said as he straightened himself.

"Yes sir, he's probably guarding his package."

"What package?"

"He was on a special drop mission."

"How do you know all this?"

"I've talked to him sir."

Tennyson paused before asking the next question. He didn't doubt Bishops accuracy because he knew the Corporal was more than competent to do his job. It was the ramifications of the incident that occupied his brain.

"What's in the package?"

"I don't know sir, he didn't tell me. But it's probably a bat scope or something like that."

"A what?"

"Bat scopes are what snipers use. It's a type of night vision."

"I see."

"He wants us to give him diplomatic immunity."

"I'm sure he does. But we can't give it to combatants, only civilians."

"Well can we bring the package in?"

"Nope, can't do that. It would look like we were in the arms trafficking business."

"Then what do we do sir?"

"God knows Corporal. But rest assured we can't give him any help. If the North found out we were protecting the enemy we'd be in a hell of a fix."

"Yes sir. I see that now."

"DO you? Do you really Corporal?" Tennyson said with all the implication he could muster.

"What are you saying sir?" Bishop asked.

The major's tone was that of a man who just blew through a toll booth without leaving the proper change.

"Remember what I said earlier about warriors getting things done?"

"Yes sir and the rest of it that they cause a lot of trouble."

"So don't cause us any trouble Corporal," Tennyson said with a wink.

"You know sir," Bishop said as he pulled the jeep back on the road. "When I joined the Canadian Army I was really hoping to be laying on some beach somewhere tossing coconuts at seagulls."

"Made you think again didn't we?"

"Ahhhh yes sir. You sure did."

CHAPTER 20

S hortly after the TET offensive of 1968 when the North tried to overrun the South, military strategists at West Point began the simulated process of a counter attack, and what it would take to end the war in Vietnam. A nobler endeavor hasn't ever been encouraged, but the flaw in the ointment was that it followed a disastrous entanglement similarly tried during the Second World War.

Like Montgomery's plan for Operation Market Garden, when Thirty Corps was to charge headlong up a single highway to Arnhem, the South would do the same. And as it was proven, the disaster occurred when allied forces couldn't reach the bridge too far. In the South's case, they too would have to capture all the bridges crossing major rivers before they could reach Hanoi.

For the South to invade the North their problem would be immediate in the sense that the only bridge that crossed into the North at the DMZ had already been destroyed years earlier. Highway 1 was the main road running the length of the country and it crossed the Ben Hai River that centered the DMZ. The Hein Luong Bridge was the only structure that could support tanks. It was obvious to both sides that the bridge would have to be raised to the ground as a deterrent. Each took turns at was more of an artillery dual then a destroy mission to accomplish the task at hand.

Once the smoke cleared, philosophically speaking, a series of frontier forts were built along the river from the coast inland to the first line of mountains not more than 30 miles from the sea. On both sides of the DMZ huge fire-support bases were constructed and several thousand men starred at each other through binoculars to see who would blink first.

As an added bonus, the North decided it would be a good idea, since Canada was there to observe violations of the Non-aggression Act of 1954, to have a front row seat as it were. And so began the establishment of Group 2, which was a former Christian church and school complex less than a thousand yards from the barbed wire fence marking the beginning of the DMZ.

The four building complex shaped like an open box was made up of a school, now used as the meeting house, a church now used as the unit dining hall and operations room, the parsonage that had no use, and the medical hospital and orphanage, also vacant. An impressive campus underutilized by the only two occupants, Private Tommy Summers and the boss, Chief Warrant Alec Harper. A narrow road connected the Group to Highway 1 and it was lined with cedar trees.

There was a small playground behind the school that now served as a landing pad for helicopters, just like the one Major Tennyson was on hours earlier. Surrounding the entire facility was gently rolling hills that were used by the locals for grazing of what few animals they had left. Between the hills during the winter months were small streams that in summer created huge swamps.

It was now just past noon and the two main tenants along with their addition, Corporal Bishop took a seat at a small table in the mess. Bishop was in the process of becoming more human like when the Major's chopper left, rotor blades washing off the tiled roofs with a light misty rain.

"Sorry Corp, all we have are the usual dry rations for chow," Tommy explained as he handed the NCO his meal.

"No sweat man," Bishop replied in his usual American slang.

"While you were changing Corporal," Alec began.

Because the Warrant and the Private were the only two observers, keeping secrets was impossible. Each man knew what the other was doing at all times, so the need for secrecy was redundant.

"Yes sir," Bishop replied taking a spoonful of condensed ham and eggs from his tin.

"Our Adjutant informed me about some of your concerns before he left. And I am to give you as much help as possible."

Bishop stopped chewing for a moment. He was taken back at what was being told him on the basis that tradition always stood in the way of expediency.

"Yes sir."

"But I'll have you know that our ability to help you is governed by our regulations which I cannot break."

"Yes sir, I understand that too."

"Good," Alec said firmly. "Now what's your plan?"

"Well as I see it we, or should I say I have two problems. The first is the downed pilot and the second is the package he was to deliver."

"So you want to get him out first eh?"

"Yes sir, because the package can be nuked, I mean destroyed."

"How you going to do that Corp?" Tommy asked with a grin.

"I'm not, the pilot is," Bishop began, then lowering his voice as if he didn't want to be overheard by nobody present, he added. "You see if we can get him back across the DMZ he'll call in an Arch light and tomorrow morning there'll be eighty acres of jungle cleared for rice paddies." Bishop said wryly. "We call it urban renewal back in the world."

Alec grinned at the comment. "So then your real problem is getting the pilot out?"

"Exactly," Bishop responded. "I figure if we can get him across the river he'll have a chance at making it to Alpha One and from there the wheels will be in motion."

"No chance at all," Alec said. "You see the American Fire base you're talking about is three miles from the river."

"So?"

"Well the way the South defends its borders is the first hundred yards from the river is covered in motion and detection sensors. From there to the firebase is the artillery and bombing zone and when you get within a hundred yards of the base it's a free fire zone. Anything out there wondering around is going to get wasted," Alec explained. "And besides, that isn't your real problem eh."

"What is?"

"Well, on this side the North has planted 80 thousand land mines along with all kinds of booby traps between the wire and the river. They've blown up more rabbits down there than the US has dropped bombs."

"Okay," Bishop commented as he considered another option. "What about this, we get him to the coast, steal a boat and he rows south."

"No chance, there's a six mile per hour current out there and it flows north. Drop him in at midnight and by morning he should be on Hainin Island. Then the Chinese can deal with him."

"Okay inland?"

"Well, you might stand a chance by following the wood cutters trails out there, but I would bet against it."

"Then the only way is to call for a chopper extraction?"

"That's the usual way," Alec said then added. "But instead of one downed pilot you may have a dozen. And not all of them alive."

"Yea, especially this close to the big D" Bishop added. "One thing's for sure, I got to get some food out to him ASAP."

"That we can help with, but don't get caught out there. They won't hesitate to shoot first and ask later."

"Right, I think I got that part real clear sir."

"So when you going Corp?" Tommy asked anxiously. He was becoming very interested in the subversive side of peacekeeping. It tended to break the monotony.

"I'll head out tonight I guess."

"Okay," Alec said. "We can put a kit together for you. We've got a spare rucksack around here don't we Tommy?"

"Right Sir. And he'll need a medical kit too."

"Just in case you step on something you shouldn't" Alec replied.

CHAPTER 21

In war, Bishop had learned the weather can be a friend or an enemy. On clear days you can see your opponent quite clearly, even though he usually is out of range. On bad days, rain, wind and darkness makes it easy to cover great distances simply because everyone is too busy trying to keep dry. And these were the conditions Bishop launched himself into later that night.

Alec and Tommy had put together a selection of things Bishop and the pilot could use to conceal themselves from a distance. Close up, there might be some problems.

Ponchos and Pith helmets, the type used by the NVA would make them blend into a jungle setting, looking like two soldiers on patrol. Also inside the rucksack were the medical kit and several ration tins. It wasn't the best food of choice, but it would keep them going. Two canteens of water and a candy bar rounded out the supplies.

It was just after eight in the evening when Bishop hopped over a six foot fence at the back of the compound.

Alec and Tommy watched in the darkness of the parsonage window as the Corporal ran along the landing pad to a small stream and disappeared into the night. With no way of contacting Bishop, the other two members could only wait it out. Neither knew how long or when Bishop would be back.

"Do you think we ought to write him up for something?" Tommy asked, considering it might be advantageous to do so if questioned later.

"On what charge?" Alec queried.

"I don't know eh. Maybe I could say I told him about a whore house up the road or something?"

"Abandoning his post might work," Alec said as the two tuned and went back to the meeting hall, and their quarters.

*   *   *

Bishop was no Chingachgook, but he did have a keen sense of direction, even in the dark. He made his way up stream along a slowly widening creek in a westerly direction. He knew the jungle wasn't that far off and once inside the tree line he could make better time because there were no patrols that close to the border. The DMZ defenses were to keep people in, and nearly everyone knew that.

Following a series of low lying hills that seemed to overlap one another, Bishop found himself coming out near a farm house. Using the out buildings as a landmark, he could just see the toughness of jungle not more than a hundred yards off.

In the darkness the high winds had now grown to nearly typhoon proportions and the noise was near deafening. Bishop slid into the protection of the double canopy rainforest and the towering trees around him served as a windbreak. At this point he was able to pick up a wood cutters trail heading north.

Bishop had made the first mile in record time for someone on foot in a strange place. Pausing by a stand of bamboo, he took out one of the canteens and slugged down a mouth full. While placing the container back inside his pack he spotted something on the ground. It was something that shouldn't be there. It was the size eleven boot print of an aviator.

Looking out across the rice paddies due east and a bit to the north he spotted the anti-aircraft base. This meant he was maybe six or seven hundred yards from the plane. Somewhat gratified by his progress Bishop started off again, this time staying within eye sight of the dike trails he had been on the day before.

Bishop rounded a small bend in the trail and there it sat. The remains of the downed plane lay prone against the splashing waves of the paddy. It was like an island unto itself, with no connection to the rest of the scene.

Moving with more adherence, he made his way to the point where he had met the pilot. Looking on the ground he spotted hundreds of boot prints, all leading away in different directions. He concluded the pilot was not staying put, but exploring his position to know where everything was. Being aware of your location was primary in any escape attempt.

But then it suddenly dawned on him. With all these prints in the wet mud it was impossible to determine which way the pilot had gone. And if the enemy had found them then they too would be puzzled and it would require a much larger force to search the area. This would also give the pilot time to escape by back tracking his own routes of departure.

"Oh shit," Bishop said his voice at normal volume.

It didn't matter how loud he spoke, the roar of the wind swept away any sound that was made.

Bishop paused to think about what the pilot had said about a place to hide. It was something about a cave being nearby. The only direction that was open was westward toward the hills and ridgelines.

Without a second thought of the improbable chance of finding a cave, and it being the right one, didn't dissuade him in the least. It wouldn't be the first time someone was lost in the jungle and he and his men had to go find them.

Turning westward Bishop began the search. His only clues were that caves generally are dugout of hillsides or along river banks. Usually they are in an open spot because the elements or diggers had stomped down the vegetation near the opening.

Of course the opening could be overgrown or even camouflaged. The difference would be if it were camouflaged the leaves of the branches would be dry and fall off or look like it had been hit with defoliant. If it were a bush of some kind in most cases it would be of a different variety of the surrounding vegetation which also stands out. In nearly all cases the cave would be used by either people of animals and they left tracks in the dirt at the mouth of the cave.

The most important clue was the size eleven flight boot. Once a few yards away from the clustering of boot prints, Bishop was able to settle on one set that went in the same direction as he was.

It took some doing to follow the prints. The muddy ground left clear imprints, but where a stream of water ran down or a low spot the prints merged with the soil and vanished. Bishop also noticed that the pilot was prone to making right turns unexpectedly, then going a few paces before turning left as if to set up an ambush. Something he had learned the hard way.

Before long the Corporal found himself standing beside a wide creek that was filling with runoff from the ridgeline farther up. The water was brown and clouded and parts of trees swept past in the current. Scanning the far bank he could only see the jungle waving happily at him as if to say, 'not this side sucker.'

He then turned and looked back the way he came and that was when he thought he saw it. A trick with night vision comes when you try to see a light far off. To look directly at it, it tends not to be where you thought it was and disappears. But by looking slightly to the left or right the light can be seen. This time the light was not like a bulb, but a glow, a yellowish glow. The kind caused by a small fire.

The dim glow became brighter the near he got to it. Glancing down he spotted the boot prints and this time they looked more recent, as if the pilot had come down to the bank to quench his thirst.

When the Corporal was close to the mouth he bent down to keep a low profile and moved slowly. Moving up beside the opening he quickly glanced in trying to not make a good target. He spotted the silhouette of a man seated with his back to the opening and the small fire in front of him.

"Captain Cook, that you?" Bishop whispered. But his voice carried into the cave like a distant echo.

Bishop could see the man still sitting there, unresponsive. Thinking the Captain was asleep, Bishop climbed up into the cave and moved cautiously. Then, just as the Corporal was to touch the Captains should Cook wheeled around with his pistol pointing into the darkness behind him. But before Cook could get a shot off Bishop grabbed the pistol between the hammer and the chamber. Cook squeezed the trigger and the hammer nailed Bishops hand between his thumb and forefinger. In a single motion Bishop lunged forward and the two feel on the fire, putting it out.

"Christ all mighty sir, what the fuck you doing?" Bishop called as the struggle suddenly stopped.

"Canook, is that you," Cook asked.

"Who the fuck you think it is and let go of the fucking gun."

An instant later the two men were sitting in the darkness inches from each other. Bishop gently pulled the hammer back and yanked his blooded hand off the firing pin.

"Here, keep that in the holster will yea," Bishop said with disgust.

"Sorry buddy, I didn't know it was you."

"That's alright sir, I guess I should have called before coming over."

They moved closer to the opening. Even the darkness of night gave more light than what was in the cave.

Bishop slipped his pack off and opened the tie down flap. Reaching in he pulled out one of ration tins and handed it to Cook followed by a canteen.

"Sorry sir, that's the best I can do."

"No problem Corporal it's a feast to me," Cook replied as he twisted the key on top of the tin and began to open the ration of food.

Moments later one had a bandaged hand while the other devoured the second ration tin.

"So what's the plain?" Cook asked between swallows.

"Moral of the story is; I'm not supposed to help you."

"Why NOT!"

"We're peacekeepers sir, not traveller's aid."

"What am I supposed to do give up?"

"Fuck no sir," Bishop replied.

"You know for a Canadian you sure don't sound like one."

"It's a long story that can wait till later. Right now I'm going to give you the shit."

"Okay Corporal, go ahead."

"Check this, I get you down South and when you get back you call in can an Arch-light on this location. You clobber the bird and your package in one dump."

Cook leaned back against the wall and put the near empty tin between his legs contemplating the solution. It made sense to a certain degree but there was a problem.

"I'm okay with you getting me back, but I don't have the package with me."

Bishop was surprised.

"So where the hell is it?"

Cook paused before answering. He wasn't completely sure about the Corporal. Bishop didn't sound Canadian; in fact he had been definitely influenced by American GI slang. But then there was the uniform and Bishop's buddy, and if the Corporal was working for the North why didn't he bring soldiers back instead of coming alone?

There is a phrase fighter pilots use when making contact with the illusive enemy and calling back to fellow fliers. 'I believe I have sighted them,' was the phrase which actually meant, I haven't seen them but I believe I know where they are. It becomes a leap of faith that has no basis in reality. None the less, it's an instinctual feeling that can't go over looked. This was the internalized feeling Cook was experiencing at that moment.

"Okay Corporal," Cook said with a sign. "The package is about a thousand yards south of here and up in the biggest dam tree in North Vietnam."

"Your shit'en me sir?"

"When I was hit by that flack gun I jettisoned the load. About fifteen seconds later I was plowing up a rice paddy."

"Oh man," Bishop said as he too leaned back against the wall.

"The drag chute only partially opened and because I was so low it hit the top of a tree and didn't come down." Cook said almost apologetically. "It's hanging up there covered in vines."

"A thousand yards you say?"

"Yup."

"Well, they're going to have to send a hell of a lot of 52's to cover that much ground."

"And probably more than once."

"And this close to the big 'D' the SAM's will knock um down like clay pigeons."

"You got it. That's why I haven't gone back south already."

"Okay, so what's your plain sir?"

"I haven't got one. All I know is that package can't end up in the wrong hands."

"What's so important about a Bat scope?"

"Bat scope! Is that what you think is in there?"

"What else could it be except some hopped up radio of some kind."

Cook was taken aback by the Corporals naivety, but then why should the Canadian think it might be something more important?

What was actually in the ten foot long container weighing 300 pounds was the prototype of new weapon that would save thousands of lives due to collateral damage. It was only a thousand yards away in one of the biggest trees in North Vietnam.

CHAPTER 22

"Hello Major Tennyson," a voice called from the crowd of dignitaries at the embassy gathering.

The Major had been ordered on short notice to make an appearance at the diplomatic function the very evening of his return from getting Bishop out of jail. He didn't really like mingling with those he had come to hate more than his own mother. The average time spent at these types of functions was usually just over an hour and he was already forty five minutes into the schmoozing time.

"Yes sir, "Tennyson replied with his hand extended in the customary greeting. "I don't believe I've met you before?"

"I'm Dmitri Pskov Commissar of the Peoples Aid Directorate of Hungary. I was just assigned here last week."

"Oh, then this is your first function?"

"No, I have been to the Uncle Hoa Banquet a few days ago and met all the North's dignitaries. At least the ones I'll be working with," Dmitri said while taking a sip from his wine glass.

The Canadian's only served campaign when the real important people came to visit, like the US envoy."

"Have they given you good accommodations?"

"To be sure. I have a lovely view of the western mountains that gives me magnificent sun sets."

"Oh good," Tennyson replied then adding. "The only view of the west we have is the apartment building across the street."

"It is unfortunate that the North didn't give you better place," Dmitri said with that kind of look that makes one feel inferior for just being alive.

"Oh well, what are you going to do?"

"Do what?"

"Sorry Dmitri. It's an expression we Canadian's use," Tennyson replied with a polite grin.

"Oh a joke yes?"

"Something like that."

Tennyson tossed back the remainder of his drink signaling to even the most ignorant person the conversation was over. But he had forgotten that nearly all politicians, even in the Warsaw Pack held little esteem for intellect and common courtesy.

"I think I'll freshen this up," Tennyson said as he tried to depart but was stopped by a firm hand on his lower arm.

"I heard you had near miss by American bombs the other day?"

"Yes that's right," Tennyson said. "The Americans may have all the guns but they still can't shoot straight."

Tennyson had learned years earlier that to make friends with those you hate you run down those you like. And the Americans were exceptional at providing that kind of ammunition.

"So then why do you work for them?"

"We don't Dmitri," Tennyson said firmly. "Those are just rumors, there is no proof!"

"My government thinks there is. I was briefed on your reports of target damage to the American Counsel in Saigon."

"Look," Tennyson replied agitated by the reference. "It's our job to make reports on breaches in the Non-Aggression Pack to the belligerent party. In this case it was the Americans. How the hell is the UN supposed to prevent these things from happening if they aren't reported?"

"Our system is more superior and direct," Dmitri argued.

"Yes of course it is that's why it doesn't work any better than ours does."

"I am apologetic Major Tennyson," Dmitri remarked. "I see your glass is empty. When it is full you may see my point?" the diplomat stated and then he turned and faded into the crowd.

"Not if I'm still sober," Tennyson muttered as he too vacated the premises for the sanctuary of his quarters in the other end of the building.

CHAPTER 23

Captain Cook was right; the package was in the tallest tree in North Vietnam Bishop concluded. As the two stood starring up at the small parts of the delivery canister just barely visible, he estimated it to be some fifty feet above them. And worse of all was the fact the closets limb to reach for was thirty feet up on the bark less tree.

It had started to rain again and the wind hadn't declined. It still was excessively noisy, but before leaving the cave Bishop had emptied the contents of his pack.

There were two ponchos and Pith Helmets typical of NVA issue which they had covered themselves with. Bishop ordered the Captain to take off his boots and walk bear footed to confuse their tracks. The Captain complied and tied the laces of his boots together so he could hang them around his neck under the poncho.

As the Captain led Bishop to the base of the tree the Corporal made every effort to step in the Captains foot prints. His smooth souled shoes obliterated the foot prints which would make it harder to follow. The officer ranks of the NVA mostly wore shoes as part of their uniform.

"So how do we get it down Corporal?"

"We're not going to sir."

"We can't leave it here."

"Why not," Bishop replied. "The winds been howling for hours and the dam thing hasn't come down. I think it's permanent up there."

"Doesn't matter. I have to get it down and buried somewhere"

"What's so damn important about that thing anyway?"

Cook paused before divulging the secret. He had no choice but to let Bishop in on some of the details of his mission. Another act of faith as it were.

"Okay, I'm not supposed to tell you this, but the equipment in side that case is a new targeting system for LGB's."

"What the hell is an LGB?" Bishop said as he knelt down to be less visible if anyone was around.

Cook knelt down beside him and replied, "LGB's are Laser Guided Bombs."

"How does that work?"

"There's a bridge about 70 miles north of here and it's called the Dragons Back. We've been pounding the crap out of it for months and not a single bomb has hit it. The reason is the attack approach run. The bridge is in a deep valley and on the bend of a river. So a plane can't make a straight on approach. In fact you have to bank to the right and toss you load at it."

"Yea," Bishop said as he thought back to what the phantom pilots did out at Khe Sanh. "It's called skip bombing isn't it?"

"That's right Corporal, but how did you know?"

"Well sir, it's because I served with the 101st Airborne during Lam Son 719 back in 1971. I was out at Khe Sanh and that's what the fly boys did. It wasn't accurate, but it sure blew the hell out of the jungle.

"You got it. Now think of one plane, one bomb and one destroyed target."

"That sounds better, a lot less risk. But how does it work?"

"Inside the package are several laser guns. They send out an infrared beam of light which is called the sparkle. Inside the nose of the bomb is a laser detection device and once it's released from the rack it looks for the sparkle and homes in. After that it's automatic," Cook explained. "And I guess you should know this too, every B-52 headed to Hanoi has at least three laser bombs in its load. There testing them as well."

"Ain't that some shit?" Bishop said almost overwhelmed by the thoughts of such accuracy.

"That's why I can't leave it."

"Yea, you got that right. But the moral of the story is you can't stay here. The longer your out banging around the chances are you're going to get picked up."

"Yea I guess you're right."

"So here's the plain. I get you back down south and when you're back you call your boss and clue him in. Let them decide what to do about this thing."

"What if the dinks find this equipment?"

"Sir, your boss doesn't know where you're at or what's happened to you. Besides that, even if the dinks do get this stuff it will take years before they figure it out. Trust me."

"You're probably right Corporal," Cook objectively concluded.

"All right. Then we head south. There's a road not far from here we can take over the ridgeline. On the other side is the Ben Hai River. Once across that your home free, in a way."

Bishop's estimated plain of simplicity would prove to be grossly over emphasized. Even with the elements concealing their movements, there were many traps to avoid, and both men were well aware the need for a colossal amount of luck.

CHAPTER 24

As the two reluctant heroes made their way south, Bishop kept his eye on the sky. The clouds were down to about a thousand feet and even with the misty rain falling he could see the reflected glow of the North's firebases in the clouds. It was like looking at a string of street lights in the sky. If he kept the skylights to his left he knew he was west of Group 2.

They travelled for about a half hour before they came to the road Bishop had found earlier. The road that came from the east rolled over a hill top and spread westward over a long flat prairie like terrain. He could just make out the start of the jungle ridgeline about a half mile westward. There was no traffic which made the going easier.

When they left the seclusion of the tree line behind them, Bishop and Cook strolled along like a couple of lost tourists. The road wasn't paved, but it had been covered over a time or two with oil which kept the dust down in summer making it hard for the South to tell how many vehicles used it during the day.

What made it uncomfortable for bear feet was the stones were lodged in the oil covering. For the most part the stones had been pounded into the surface by the hundreds of vehicles crossing over it. But occasionally it had long smooth parts too. So anyone in bear feet had to constantly keep an eye open for the smooth parts if they wanted to get very far.

This of course wasn't a problem for peasants; their feet were so heavily callused it didn't bother them.

Even though the landscape was fairly flat Bishop didn't see the dip in the road and wasn't aware until they were just about to head down the steep incline. Pausing, the Corporal motioned for Cook to take cover in a clump of bushes nearby.

"Wait here," Bishop ordered and slowly started down the road.

He hadn't gone but a hundred feet when he heard the unmistakable sound of rain pulverizing a tin roof. Peering through the fog of mist he could just make out a small building in a cluster of bamboo trees just off the road to his right. Looking beyond, Bishop could see the road disappear over a second dip and then up the backside of the hill. But through the middle of the depression he spotted creek water flowing like the wind.

It was then two guards came out of the small building and out onto the road. Bishop stood like a granite post not moving an inch. Instinctively he knew that the backdrop of the blackened road and covered in a poncho would be a natural cover for him. In addition the guards were some distance away and in the rain he would not be easy to see.

The guards stood in the road for a moment as if not sure why they were out on such a night and then turned west. They went on until they reached the top of the depression, stood for a moment observing what looked like the rising creek water, and then returned to shack.

During this like interruption Bishop stayed right where he was. When the guards went back inside he took a few steps backward and then went back to rejoin Captain Cook.

"What's up?" Cook asked nervously.

"We got to make a detour around a guard house up ahead."

"Okay," Cook replied and then headed back into the jungle.

"Wait a minute," Bishop said as he reached out and grabbed Cook by the arm.

"What's the problem? Well just use the woods for cover and go around them."

"First rule of camouflage," Bishop said. "Look like you belong there."

The two huddled back into the bushes and got low to the ground.

"What time is it?" Bishop asked.

Cook glanced at his watch, "about 21:46 hours," which in human time means 10:46 PM.

"We'll wait a little bit."

"What for?"

"Guards change at ten."

Cook nodded and shifted himself to be more comfortable on the rain soaked ground. It was getting cold because they had stopped walking and the sweat under the ponchos cooled the skin in the damp air.

Bishop bent forward enough to see the crest of the road to the east back lit by the glow of the firebases. It was if on cue that he spotted several shadows on bicycles drifting closer on the shiny blacktop.

"This shouldn't take long," Bishop said as he lowered himself into the concealment.

There were about a dozen of them, all covered in ponchos and wearing pith helmets. The gusting elements whipped their faces and all kept their heads bowed to the storm.

An officer was leading the squad and he was wearing long trousers that hung below his rain gear. The group cycled right passed the two foreigners hiding in the brushes completely unaware of the men's position.

At the hut the group clustered and dropped their cycles in the grass next to the door. The barrier opened and the group pushed their way inside eager to take shelter.

A few minutes elapsed and a second group flowed outside. Taking up enough two wheel transportation the relieved sentinels headed back towards Cook and Bishop. Like before the group went by and disappeared over the crest of the hill.

But this time Bishop made a count of the returnees. There were only nine. Where were the others, or even were there others, became the question of the day?

"Now what?" Cook whispered.

Bishop said nothing. Instead he motioned for Cook to follow him. They went back into the jungle line and moved closer to the hut. They took up a position close enough to hear the voices of the men inside laughing at something.

Cook looked at his watch and then over at Bishop.

"Ten Past."

Bishop nodded but didn't make attempt to move. It seemed like an hour went by when the door opened and three more guards left the hut. Snatching up the remaining bikes they headed back up the road.

"Okay, now," Bishop whispered and the two broke from cover and went around the back of the building.

When they reached the corner of the hut closest to the road Bishop almost fell over them in the grass. There were four more cycles laying there.

"Judas Priest," Bishop whispered and motioned for Cook to drop back into the darkness.

"Where the hell did they come from?" Cook asked softly.

"Beats the fuck out of me but we ain't wait'en," Bishop said and headed for the prone cycles.

With Cook following like a trained monkey the two snatched up a bike each and slid them onto their shoulders. Once on the road they headed for the creek.

Bishop and Cook trotted down into the water and hustled through the stiff current as fast as they could. It was waste deep and Bishop noted that the North had pounded large polls into the creek bottom beside the underwater roadway to make it look like a bombed out crossing. He wasn't the only one who knew about concealment.

On the far bank the two men scrambled up the incline and once clear they hopped on board their conveyance and started peddling like hell into the darkness.

Before them lay the ridgeline and they could see the road making a turn to the left before starting up the hill. Even from their position the road looked steep and straight. No turns or flat spots to catch your breath on.

"Don't steer in a straight line sir," Bishop said as he wheeled close to his partner.

"Why not?"

"We're not practicing formation flying sir. We're supposed to look like a couple of idiots."

"Okay got it," Cook replied and began the practice of sporadic zigzagging of the wheel.

Bishop watched and shortly became comfortable with the fact they did look like a couple of idiots.

As they came into full view of the upward bound road Bishop spotted a secondary road intersecting from the right. It looked like it was coming right out of the jungle and the opening was barely visible.

"Keep peddling don't stop," Bishop commanded.

Cook complied and kept his head down so his face couldn't be seen. Had he looked up and to his right he would have spotted what his partner did.

Stretched between the upper branches of the trees were huge camouflage nets and under them a truck park for tanks and anti-aircraft tractors. If it hadn't been raining the wet vehicles would have not given off a glinting of nightlight.

"Shit," Bishop whispered. "They must have half the NVA armored division in there."

Cook said nothing and concentrated on his maneuvering.

They made the turn at the bottom of the hill and started the climb. Like two decathloner's in the last hundred feet of the race, they pushed hard and slipped into the darkness of the upward road.

CHAPTER 25

Maps of Hanoi were not readily available from local venders, and the one Sergeant Wilkins had pinned to his wall of his quarters was the size of an opened newspaper. What made this map different was all the main sections of the city had been traced around. The Old Quarter, the French Quarter, the Lake District and alike had been bordered in red pencil. The sergeant also added in gray pencil the areas that were continuously hit by American bombing missions.

Wilkins room wasn't very large and included a desk and chair, a wardrobe that sat in one corner and his bed which he had shoved lengthways against the wall. It gave the room the illusion of being larger than it was. A small tattered rug made of towel strips which he had purchased at the local market held down the center of the floor. Accept for the map, there was only one other picture and it was of Prime Minister Trudeau.

The simple task of deduction would have been the same if you lowered the IQ and raised the average age of an officer. What tends to happen when the problem is rationalized by the mainstream observer is that the solution becomes more evasive the longer you gaze at it. Like staring into an empty glass of beer, it wasn't going to get filled on its own.

What Wilkins kept running through his mind is what Pogozinski had said about needing a dry place to do the printing in. This made a great deal of sense to the sergeant because it was logical. Obviously if you're going to print counterfeit money it would have to be in a safe and dry place.

What wasn't logical was the map before him and the tracings. Except for the near miss during the last raid a couple of days ago that wouldn't of happened had Bishop been on his toes, all the severely bombed out areas were south of the Red

River. North of their location was also heavily bombed. And when he took in to consideration the occasional flooding, this too eliminated several large swaths of real estate. Most of which was down town.

He climbed from his bed and walked over to the window. His view was south easterly and he could see most of the tall buildings, the highest was only four floors. Looking up he could see the glow of city lights against the low gray clouds. The reflection made it easy to see the shadowy structures surrounding the compound. He then noticed the large chunk of missing roof from the building that took the bomb hit. Some five blocks distance wasn't enough to save having to replace most of the windows on that side of the chateau.

Stepping back he drifted to his bunk and lay down again with his left arm supporting his head on the pillow.

He began to stare at the map again. This time he plotted Group 6, the Embassy and the airport. He picked the airport simply because it was the closest destination that could handle large shipments near the city. Wilkins was counting on the fact that the special paper for making money had to be flown in and then transferred to the printing press.

A curiosity began to press on his mind. Why would the money be printed here in Hanoi? What if it was printed somewhere else and just brought here? The answer to both questions he concluded would be security. If the North was going to ship bogus money to the South, keeping it close to the source of conspirators would be necessary.

This answer brought forth another question and it ended up being the same as the first. Where would you put a printing press and all that goes with it?

As Wilkins began to labor over the possibilities he surmised it would have to be somewhere that wouldn't draw attention, and yet busy enough to go unnoticed. It also had to be a place where people gathered in mass so an air strike would be out of the question, even for the Americans. It had to be a place like the down town market. It suited most of the needs except for a building large enough to house the operations. There was nothing of that nature in close proximity.

"Judas Priest," Wilkins muttered. "Something like that could be anywhere, even in the citadel."

From beyond his closed door the sergeant could hear footsteps shuffling around in the hall. The movement was familiar; it meant one of the Privates was headed to the bathroom at the end of the corridor.

Rolling over, Wilkins pulled his bed sheet up over him and faded off to sleep.

CHAPTER 26

For two soldiers who are supposed to be in top physical condition, they collapsed on the crest of the ridgeline, just as the road went over and down the back side at the opposite angle. Cook and Bishop had tossed their bicycles against the side of the road and they lay prone on their backs in the low brush while the rain washed the sweat from their foreheads.

"How the hell do they get up here?" Bishop gasped.

"No wonder they're so damn hard to kill," Cook replied.

The two took a short respite before Bishop climbed to his feet and helped Captain Cook to stand. Together they pulled their two wheel transport from the mud and started down the incline.

Bishop led the way and before going more than a hundred feet he spotted a break in the embankment where obvious foot traffic had made a permanent connection with the road. He halted the Captain and freed himself from his bike. Looking over the edge he could see the trail taper its way into the tree line of the jungle.

"Just what we need sir," Bishop said with a grin. "A way south."

The two carried their cycles on their shoulders along the trail to where it entered the jungle. Placing their bikes within a stand of bamboo which was out of sight from the road, they began to follow the wood cutters trail as it led deeper into the undergrowth.

The trail was made up of wide parts and narrower ones indicating the harvest of trees. The wider parts were open as if the two were crossing a broad field and then shrunk to a single line as it careened across out cropping's and slope lines.

The wind and rain had subsided on the back side of the ridge line. The second line of hills to the west was also similarly quiet. It was if they had walked into an

97

indoor garden with an open roof. Vegetation still wiggled around and light rain still pattered away, but on the whole the walk was less restrictive.

Part way down the hillside, the two came across a small tin hut parked under a huge Cedar tree. Bishop knew it was the supply shack the cutters used to store tools and alike. When with the Americans he had come across similar huts while on patrol. They were never a threat and made a good place to dry out in.

"Check it out sir. We'll sit in here for a while and rest," Bishop said as he made for the shelter.

Once inside Cook and the Corporal found half cut logs to sit on. On the ground beside the wall Bishop found a wooden ammo box with nine inch nails and a couple of hammers. Some lengths of rope hung from a rafter against the back wall, and even in the dark it was easy to see them once their eyes became accustom to the light.

"Wonder what they use this for," Cook asked while taking a handful of spikes from the wooden box.

"Hang up their hats," Bishop commented jokingly.

The Corporal knew what they were for but made no attempt to inform the Captain.

When Bishop was on patrol he discovered the real reason behind the nails and hammers. When taking down a huge tree in the jungle making a clean cut at the base of the trunk created more problems than necessary. As a result the wood cutters would drive nails into the side of the trunk and using lengths of rope to hold themselves close, they would drive the nails in forming a ladder to the top. Once there, they would cut out all the larger limbs that would snag on the surrounding trees and vines. When finished they would cut the base of the tree and it would fall as a clean log missing any hang ups.

It was then that Bishop heard a familiar sound echoing through the trees. The rush of water over a falls indicated they were less than a few hundred yards for the DMZ border. The falls was actually on the Ben Hai River which flowed south through the valley before turning east to form the center line of the DMZ. It was also where a tributary of the Cam Loa River merged to form a wye and not far from the wye was the abandon fire base known as Khe Sanh. A place Bishop was all too acquainted with.

"Come on sir, were almost home," Bishop said with a grin.

As before Bishop led the way with the Captain not more than a few paces behind. The wind gusted enough to cover any sounds the two made and travel was more a leisure than a challenge.

At the river they turned south and followed the bank passed the crescendo of falling water beyond a churning pool and down to the fork Bishop knew was there. Taking cover in the bushes directly in front of the merging rivers, the two paused to rest. The going had been easy but tiring due to the huge boulders that lined the banks.

"I think it's around here somewhere, "Bishop whispered.

"What?"

"The underwater bridge."

"You kidding?"

"Nope," the Corporal continued has he related his story from the past.

"When I was at Khe Sanh I was on a patrol that was following some sappers that used to hit us at night. We tracked then down to that side of the river, but by the time we got here the dinks were gone. We never could figure out how they crossed over until we caught one a few weeks later. He told us of that bridge you can't see from the sky."

Cook was awed by Bishop's tail but it had a definite ring of truth to it. He was now confident that he was in the right hands. And Canadian sounding or not, Bishop was fully cognizant of his facts.

"Stay here," Bishop ordered as he slipped out onto the river bank.

The water was higher due to the runoff and the normal muddy bank was below the surface. Here and there flat rocks looked like small islands holding on for dear life. Crouched on each stone Bishop began to toss small pebbles out into the river. He was listening for the distinct sound of shallow water. The difference between a splash and cur-plunk gave the secret way.

After several unsuccessful probes the sound he was waiting for made itself known. Stepping down off the flat rock he found himself in knee high water. Reaching in the cold river he felt around for the cable of wire that ran to the opposite side. Once discovered, he yanked it free from the river bottom. But the wire didn't break the surface. Fortunately there was enough slack to hold onto as they crossed over.

Signaling Cook, the Captain made his way along and joined Bishop.

"Told ya it was here," Bishop said with pride in his recollection. "Hold onto this and shuffle your way across. Just follow me."

The current of the wide river was strong and the temperature near numbing. With freedom in sight Cook stayed up with the Corporal foot for foot.

Once on the opposite side the two dragged themselves from the water. It was only four hundred feet across, but the flow of water drained nearly all the strength for both men.

"Okay, now what?" Cook asked as they huddled in a thick growth of palm leaves.

"Now we find a sensor."

"A what?"

"The South doesn't mine its banks; instead it lays out thousands of noise sensors. These things are so good you can here rabbits fucking a quarter mile out."

"What do they look like?"

"It looks like a pipe with fake plastic leaves on it," Bishop replied as he started searching for the electrical informant.

As the two began their search, the rain picked up again and so too the wind. They were in the hollow of the river valley and the elements were predominant in this location.

Finding something that was designed to blend with the jungle wasn't easy, but the inventors had over looked one significant fact. Plastic, when it's wet shines differently than a living plant. And if it's just been recently replaced it smells different too.

Bishop scoured the path that led up from the bank, moving leaves and palms aside enough to see what lay underneath. He was near the top of the bank when he heard the sound of water tapping away at something metallic. Following the noise he found one of the sensors.

"Captain," Bishop whispered through the reverberation. "Up here."

Cook moved away from the bank and joined the Corporal.

"Here's one," Bishop said like a kid on an Easter egg hunt.

Cook knelt down and looked over the plastic leaves attached to the pipe. He couldn't see anything that would indicate it was a device of any kind.

"Right here sir," Bishop said as he tapped twice on what looked like the center of a flower. The sound made a popping noise.

"You're kidding me," Cook said.

"Nope, this is your ticket home sir," Bishop said. "Do you know Morris Code?"

"Yea, why?"

"Just start tapping out SOS and help is on the way."

Bishop had a wide grin on his face. The kind that gives tired people a new sense of hope.

Even though the Corporal wasn't going to be in on the rescue, he knew the certainty of it wouldn't be long in coming. The South where constantly alert for any disturbance in their vigil.

From under his poncho Bishop took out his rucksack and took the pith helmet off Cooks head. As if by silent command, Cook also removed his poncho and sat in the mud putting on his size eleven flight boots. Before the Captain had laced up his walking ware Bishop was already set for the return trip.

"Got to run sir, good luck," Bishop said as he turned and vanished into the dark.

Cook had already started his coded message for help. Sitting there in the rain and wind he wondered who Bishop really was. The descriptive word extraordinary came to mind as he watched a blackened shape slip through the current of the river. A man of this nature, Cook thought, would have to be reported to his superiors along with the location of the irretrievable package.

CHAPTER 27

'It's always the same,' Bishop thought as he made his way back along the trails to the wood cutters shack. Retreat seemed much faster when he observed the same passage in reverse.

He spent little time once inside the mall shack. It wasn't essential to take in all the details, only the ones he needed. A length of rope, a hammer and two handfuls of nine inch nails were all that was required for the next part of the self-declared mission. After storing the tools in his ruck sack he slid the door shut and continued to the next location. It was the bamboo grove by the road where the bikes were hidden.

Hours of darkness in the jungle, is a perplexing thing in the sense that sounds and darkness tend to exaggerate what is really there. What may sound like a tank coming down the road may only be a bicycle with a bent rim that rubs against the tire. The squeak and clunk are nearly identical if you let your mind wonder enough.

Bishop's mind had learned to control such a natural instinct and as a result he tended to wait it out, rather than get excited and give away his position. This was especially true when he and his men were setting up an ambush.

Dug in as it were beside his mode of transportation, he watched as a group of NVA soldiers on bicycles headed down the declining road after making the turn at the summit. Out of alignment wheels and peddles hitting the frame, gave the impression that something bigger was passing by.

When the way was clear, Bishop pulled his bike, leaving Cook's back in the trees, out onto the road.

Hopping on he cycled the short incline, made the turn and was nearly out of control heading down the back side. As he gained speed he stood on the break as hard as he could. The bike slowed then sped up as he hit one dry patch after another.

Near the bottom he could make out the driveway that went into the truck park and this time he brought his bicycle to a halt at the intersection. Looking like he was checking his bike for any problems he peered into the camouflaged storage area.

It wasn't just a truck park Bishop was observing, but a multi-unit transportation Battalion complete with flatbed trucks and armored support tanks. The positioning of the vehicles was such that it implied immediate escape. But there was no sign of anyone to drive them. No barracks, or offices or even a guard shack were present. Bishop guessed that it was an over flow area.

This was common for the North. They had a specific declaration to conceal everything military even paper clips if they were green.

It was impossible to get closer simply because, even though he looked like a soldier headed to his post, wandering into such a facility unannounced was suicide. Instead he made a mental note of the location and continued on his way.

Just as before the creek had swollen a bit more, but the crossing was less hazardous because of the floating limbs hugging the pilings that decoyed the destroyed bridge. The limbs acted as a dam of sorts and wading through the water was only tricky when he stepped into a flow that pushed harder on his body. Luckily the crossing wasn't more than seventy feet and it didn't take long to make it to the other side.

Peddling as fast as he could he slipped by the guard shack just minutes before the change over and slid into the same clustering of bushes he and Cook hid in before. Leaving his bike well covered in long grass, Bishop headed back to the biggest tree in North Vietnam and the package lodge in the top.

It was nearly morning when the Corporal found the tree again. He had actually walked passed it before realizing he had gone too far. The clue was he spotted the wrecked plane in the paddy beside the trail.

With the rain picking up again, Bishop slipped off his pack and pulled out the tools he stole from the wood cutters shack. Knowing that the pounding of hammer to nail would be difficult to conceal even in the threatening weather, he picked up a large stick and used it as a hammer. Wood against nail was less noisy and it tended to punch holes into the wood.

With the length or rope securing him to the side of the tree, he began his climb to the top. He had the foresight to pick up several wooden hammers and stuck them in his pack. As he went through one he tossed it away and used another. To speed things along he stretched out the gap between the nails he used as climbing stakes. This was a very dangerous practice, but it brought him closer to the lowest limb sooner.

"Damn," Bishop said as he pulled himself into the crotch of the branch.

He sat there looking up and he could make out the canister and shroud lines to the parachute not more than forty feet away. The trunk and limbs were wet, but with no bark on them they were easy to climb.

As he got closer to the top of the tree Bishop made quicker progress. The limbs were closer together and he found himself acting like Tarzan when swinging his way through the cluster of vines that held the canister.

It was like climbing into a huge catcher's mitt. The vines had over the years woven a tremendous pocket from which anything landing in it would be stuck there for an eternity. Bishop had no concern for falling simply because of the thickness of the vines.

Taking out a pocket knife, Bishop began cutting the shroud lines from the canister to the parachute. It was hard going because the blade wasn't designed to cut nylon of such strength and on top of that they were wet. None the less, Bishop had separated the container from the chute. What was curious was the container weighed less than a hundred pounds. It was either that or the adrenaline in the Corporal was making him feel like superman. In one momentous shove he managed to find a hole large enough in the vines to drop the canister through.

There was a terrible clanking sound when the gray container hit the rocky ground below. Not only did it land hard but rolled slightly banging off each protruding stone. But luck was on the Corporals side when the canister rolled hard and slammed against a large boulder that sprung open the casing.

"Hot Damn, we got it now," Bishop said with glee.

Coming down the tree was easier, but he managed to get his hand bleeding again. It wasn't much of a wound, but because his heart was pounding from all the exertion blood loss was considerable.

The canister was designed like a camera box. It was ten feet long, three feet thick and four feet wide with smooth sides to cut down on air drag when it hung from the bottom of the wing. The inside was specially made of foam segments that held the type of equipment it was designed to carry. Even if the canister didn't have a drag chute to slow its decent to the ground, the foam could take the full shock of impact.

Bishop knelt over the container like a vulture picking over its pray. As he looked at the objects inside the foam casement, he pulled on his bandage with his teeth enough to stop the bleeding.

There were eight of them in all. The infrared guns and battery packs the size of a shoe box laid out one over the other as if they were meant to be connected.

Bishop reached in a pulled out one of the guns. It was a funny shape and looked more like a timing light for tuning up a car motor. The difference was that one end of it had a red lens on it. Holding it like a pistol, the red lens was the part you pointed at the target. It was then he noticed the connecting port in the handle.

Retrieving one of the battery packs he found a wire with a special connector that fit the port. It was so simple a child could make it work. But the devastation Captain Cook said it was capable of was beyond child's play.

Bishop slid off his pack and snatched up two of the guns and battery packs. Placing them inside, he put his pack back on and dragged the canister to a new location tossing limbs and grass over it to conceal the location.

In an hour he would be back at Group 2 and ready for a long sleep.

CHAPTER 28

The transition from night to day under over cast skies is an indirect one. It doesn't break, but fade. For anyone watching, it plays tricks with the mind in such a way that the experience takes stages of awareness. The awareness comes when the eye blinks, and the half conscious mind realizes something's changed.

Bishop was extremely tired when he climbed over the six foot fence that was part of the Group 2 compound. The buildings were dark and it appeared as if Alec and Tommy were still asleep. He made his way to an open window that he knew was in his room and climbed through.

Sitting on the side of his bed he pulled off his muddy shoes and tossed them in the corner. He then took of his pack and placed it against the wall beside a small trunk used for storing his other uniforms, if he had any. He was in the middle of taking off his shirt when Alec knocked on his door and walked in like he owned the place.

"Mission accomplished I presume?"

"Yes sir," Bishop replied with a grin, he then shivered from the cold.

"Where's the pilot?"

"He should be home by now."

"You didn't leave him out there did you?"

"Not exactly sir, I got him across the river and then I left him," Bishop replied taking his blanket off his bunk and rapping it around himself.

"How will we know he made it back?"

"Guess when the Air Force does some urban renewal out there in the paddies."

There was a slight commotion beyond the door to Bishop's room. It sounded like somebody fumbling around in the dark.

"So your back eh?" Tommy said as he entered the Corporals quarters.

"You got it Sherlock."

"What happed to your hand?" Tommy asked as he looked at the stained bandage.

Bishop stood in the center of the room outlining his overnight adventure. He didn't feel like he was being interrogated but rather performing the duty of sharing information. During the discussion, he brought out one of the laser targeting devices and explained how it worked based on what Captain Cook had told him.

It came as no surprise to Bishop how much Tommy and Alec were amazed by the advancement of American weaponry. Neither one knew of such a development and kept expressing astonishment as Bishop hooked up the devices for a test run.

"So now what Corp?" Tommy asked.

"As I see it, we have to get this somewhere safe for the moment," Bishop replied.

"Where might that be?" Alec queried.

"I'd say the safest place would be the embassy wouldn't you sir?"

"Yes, that's right but how are you going to get it there?"

"I figure the two would fit inside a diplomatic pouch."

"We don't get pouches down here very often Corp. Not much to report on," Tommy said firmly.

Bishop stepped over to the door then crossed over to the window he had come through. Looking out into the gathering morning he could see the sky had remained overcast, but the wind and rain had gone missing.

"Alright, so what if Tommy here came down with tonsillitis? How would you get him to the hospital?

"Well," Alec began pondering the implications of a medical emergency. "I'd have to call the base camp up the road and have the doc come down and look at him. IF, he needs to go to the hospital they'll fly him to one," Alec replied.

"That's cool now have you got any explosives around here?"

"Hey wait a minute," Tommy said. "I'm not sick."

"I know you aren't but I will be."

Alec stood firm not sure what Bishop was up to, and the only way to find out was to play along.

"I don't believe we have any do we Tommy?"

"Well sir, there are those claymore's we confiscated from the basecamp last year," the Private said as he recalled the illegal use of foreign demolitions on the North's border.

"Where are they?" Bishop asked.

"In a box in the garage."

"Good."

"You're not planning on blowing us up to get to the hospital are you?" Alec said with contempt.

"No sir, I just need a little C-4 out of the back on the mine," Bishop said. "Then I'll look like I need to go to the hospital. I want you to call the basecamp and get the doc down here. I'll take care of the rest."

Like actors on a stage getting ready for the curtain to rise, the three went into action. Tommy went and got one of the claymore mines and Alec called the base Doctor who would be there in twenty minutes. They reconvened in Bishop's room.

"That thing won't work," Tommy confessed as he handed Bishop the mine. "It's rusted inside."

"No problem," Bishop replied as he smacked the mine on the corner of his trunk and cracked the plastic casing. He pulled hard and the back of the device came open.

With a finger he pulled out a chunk of the explosive and began to roll it into a small ball the size of a marble.

"This stuff is good for three things," Bishop said. "Setting off the mine, heating up your C rations, and getting off guard duty."

The Corporal explained how when he was in the jungle and it was raining, all he had to do was take a handful of C-4 and set it on fire. It burnt intensely and holding his rations over it gave him a hot meal.

The second use, which is what he really wanted it for was if you swallowed a small chunk of the explosive in ten minutes you looked like death with gray skin color and black tongue. Rounding out the charade were occasional bouts of vomiting. The only problem was it wore off in half an hour so timing was everything.

With Bishop tucked in his bed and soaked with water from a canteen to make it look like he was sweating profusely, all the others had to do was wait.

Alec and Tommy had just started eating breakfast when they heard the truck from the basecamp pull up in the courtyard.

"Well private, here we go," Alec said as he rose and went to the door.

Opening the barrier Alec was met by Doctor Chung, a North Korean. The doctor was almost as big as Alec with a broad face and deep cheek bones. His dark hair was cut in a military style and he was dressed in the North's uniform bearing the rank of Major.

"Where sick man?"

"In his room doctor," Alec said and led the officer to Bishop's quarters.

There wasn't a light in Bishop's room if he needed any it would come from a Coleman lantern kept in the outer room.

Bishop moaned when he spotted the doctor and flinched just a bit for good measure.

The doctor sat down on the side of his bunk and pulled the blanket way to see his patient in a bath of sweat. Bishop's skin color was pale and his face looked hideous.

Pressing on Bishop's stomach the Corporal gave out with a scream of fake pain.

"Oh Christ doc that hurts," Bishop moaned as he rolled into the fetus position.

"You drink much alcohol?"

Bishop nodded.

The doctor reached over and tried to get the Corporal to lie flat, but Bishop resisted as much as he dared. The doctor then pressed around the top of his kidneys and Bishop called out in pain again.

"Okay, you got liver disease," Chung said as he rose up and faced Alec.

"Anything you can do Major?" Alec asked sadly.

"No, he need surgeon. I send for airlift to Hanoi. They treat him there."

"Thanks Doctor," Alec replied.

With that, the Major left the room so quickly they could almost feel the suction.

"Dam it worked eh?" Tommy laughed. "I got to remember this one."

Once the congratulating subsided Bishop resettled himself in his bunk for a quick nap. Alec and Tommy played the role of concerned soldiers and waited for the helicopter they knew would come to land on the small field beside their camp. Seated at their table finishing their morning rations they would glance at each other and chuckle.

"Ain't he something," Tommy would say.

Alec snickered and kept eating.

Tommy finished his rations first and took up his tray and glass and went to the make shift sink to wash up. As the lowest rank he was more of the officer's aid than a private. While washing his glass he glanced out the window and spotted six men dressed in NVA uniforms walking up from the helicopter pad. The group was led by Captain Tri Hoc of the Regional Police Force. The same officer that had arrested Bishop two days earlier.

"Judas Priest sir, it's the gray mice!"

Alec leaped from his seat and nearly choked on his food.

"Where?"

"Coming up from the pad!"

"Right, take it easy and we'll get through this," Alec said and headed for Bishop's room.

The Corporal was nearly asleep when Alec burst in like a runaway bull. In two steps Alec was beside the bed shaking it frantically.

"What the fuck!" Bishop called.

"The local cop is here and he might be trouble. So look sic again."

Bishop hopped out of bed as Alec went back to the outer room and played for time. The Corporal took out of the targeting devices from his pack and looked around to see where he could hide it. Glancing up he spotted the ceiling beams were thick enough to hide his package. Standing on his bed he placed the device on the beam and then climbed back into bed.

Bishop was just pulling the cover up when Tri Hoc entered the room surround by his men holding AK-47's at the ready.

"Ah Corporal, your officer say you sick?" the Captain said as he stood beside the bed.

Bishop snapped into character and gave a mournful reply.

Hoc looked around the room searching for evidence. He and his men found some ones tracks in the mud out in the jungle along with wood cutters tools at the base of a large tree. It took some doing but the prints were traced back to the Group 2.

It was then that Hoc spotted Bishops wet and muddy shoes in the corner. Walking over the Captain picked up one of the shoes.

"You outside camp last night?"

"No sir," Bishop muttered, still playing the role of suffering soldier.

Dropping the shoe he picked up the shirt which was still wet, a small puddle of water lay on the floor below it.

"I think you lie," Hoc said casually as if he was holding all the cards.

"I'm afraid that can't be sir," Alec chimed in. "The Corporal's been here all night."

"I don't think so. We follow tracks here and those shoes made them."

Alec froze. He didn't know what to say that would be a reasonable explanation.

Hoc motioned to his men and two guards began to yank Bishop from his bed.

"Hold on sir," Alec said. "This man is protected by diplomatic immunity."

"No diplomats out here Chief Warrant." Hoc said

"Give me a break will ya?" Bishop said as he forced himself out of the guard's hands and sat on his bunk. "I'm sick sir. Ask the doc?"

"You not look good. Won't last long in my jail."

"Can I have a word with you in private sir?"

"You tell truth now?"

"Yes sir, but only to you," Bishop gasped.

Alec gave a curious look as the Captain ordered the group of men from the room and closed the door.

"You know why I'm down here don't you sir?"

"Yes, Major Tennyson told me."

"What he probably didn't tell you was that plane that got shot down had something important in it."

"We got everything in plane, no secret."

"Oh yea," Bishop said as he rose and took the pack from the wall and tossed it on his bunk. "Look inside."

Hoc wasn't sure what to expect. He had dealt with the Group 2 team on many occasions but they were always so secretive to the point of absurdity. But the Corporal seemed different in many ways.

Pulling open the top flap Hoc reached inside and took out the remaining target device and battery pack.

"Ever see anything like that before?"

Hoc said nothing as he tried to figure out what he was holding.

"Let me show you," Bishop said as he plugged the line from the battery into the port on the gun. Pointing at the wall he squeezed the trigger and instantly a small red dot appeared on the plaster. Hoc went over to investigate and tried to rub the red dot from the plaster wall.

"It doesn't come off," Bishop said as he released the trigger.

"Now check this out," Bishop began. "You want to take out a target you just press the trigger and the US Air Force dose the rest."

Hoc's eyes widened like bright lights on a motorcycle. He didn't know what he had but he knew it must be worth something.

"So you take this and give it to your Russian buddies, and let them figure it out."

Hoc walked over and took the gun from Bishop. He pointed at the wall again and the same result occurred.

"So you tell your boss you found this thing and you might get a raise in pay," Bishop coaxed.

"What you want for this?"

"I just want a ride to a hospital before I die," Bishop said as he flopped over onto his bunk.

Although Bishop's skin color was beginning to change, in the darkened room he still felt confident the exchange would go through.

Hoc stood beside the bed as if not sure what to do. All that Bishop had told him made sense and the find of new targeting equipment, even if it took years for the Soviet's to figure out, was worth the risk. If nothing else, he might be able to swing a transfer farther away from the DMZ which would make his wife happy.

The Captain took the gun and battery pack and holding it like a new born left the building taking his men with him. His mission as he saw it was to turn in his find, but to do it with the right officer to insure due credit.

"So they got it eh?" Tommy said as he ran into Bishops quarters.

"One of them, yea," Bishop replied as he lay on his back looking up at the beam over his bunk. He could just see the end of the second gun sticking out. And as he lay there, he could hear the sound of rotor blades headed his way.

CHAPTER 29

The news that their Yankee was back and in a Hanoi hospital helped Sergeant Wilkins to breathe easier. Not much was known except Bishop looked worse than he felt, and that wasn't saying a lot about a man who nearly destroyed Group 6 almost a week earlier.

Wilkins had received his 'laundry is ready' call from the embassy supply orderly and the coded message only meant that a meeting was required at the usual place, the Krakow Club.

It was nearly three in the afternoon, the normal time the Polish Contingent made its raid on the tiny tavern. Wilkins was sitting in his Lada about a half block from the pub and he had a good view of the door. His plan was to wait for Sergeant Pogozinski and his chums to wander in and then he would follow a few minutes later.

The street was occupied but not busy and to pass the time Wilkins began counting the covered air raid shelters that were nothing more than circular cement pipes used in sewers buried upright in the sidewalk. Civilians would only have to dive into the holes for protection from shrapnel and debris.

By the time he got to eighteen Wilkins was nearly broadsided by another Lada looking very much like his own. In the driver seat was Sergeant Pogozinski who looked like he had just been accused of stealing it.

"Follow ME!" the Polish NCO called as he sped off.

The Canadian was astonished when he instinctively hit the starter button and the motor revved up immediately. Crunching the gears Wilkins shot off at speed to catch his opposite counterpart.

The chase was comprised of several turns up narrow streets then rounded some monument to Uncle Hoa to end in an alley inside a narrow garage behind a restaurant. And before Wilkins could get out, Pogo was knelt down beside his door.

"What the hell is going on?" Wilkins complained.

"KGB Colonel show up a few days ago. He bring lots of company and when that happens we get to see countryside."

"Where are you going?"

"Don't know. Big surprise, even for KGB."

"They're following you aren't they?"

"Da, I mean yes comrade," Pogo replied hastily.

It was evident by his demeanor that the Russian Secret Police had the Polish Sergeant shock up. Even in foreign countries behind the iron curtain the presence of the 'leather coat gang' could mean serious trouble for anyone on their list.

Reaching over into the back seat Wilkins took out a legal tan envelope and handed it to the Pol.

"It's what you asked for last time."

"Good," Pogo said as he pulled the flap back far enough to see the Canadian Embassy letterhead on the top of the few pages inside. He would pass it up the chain to Moscow to forge the letter asking for the combine demonstration to be held up until the Polish Government had a chance to show off their equipment. The sales of farm machinery to the North was very lucrative to the country that got the contract.

"Now I have something for you," Pogo said as he leaned closer to Wilkins. "Yesterday my men join the Hungarians at train depot. Special cargo come to Hanoi from China. Lots of Chezk words printed on boxes. One box broken and inside a big printing machine. Take six men to move."

"Where in the depot?"

"In basement," Pogo paused as he searched for the right words. "Where you take cargo!"

"The freight house?" Wilkins asked knowing that freight and mail were usually handled in the same building.

"Da!" Pogo replied with an approving grin. "Now you go, I smell Ruski!"

Wilkins nodded and slapped the shifter into reverse. With a jolt he was backed out of the garage and headed up the alley. As he turned into the street he glanced in his rear view mirror and spotted Pogo roaring up behind.

When the Pol hit the same street he went in the opposite direction.

Wilkins wondered if he would see his only contact with the Warsaw Pack contingent again. He did know that Pogo was a survivor and a good soldier, even if he did go behind his bosses back. But that was a sign of the times then, and probably would remain so far into the future.

CHAPTER 30

The problem with being a patient in the North's hospital was it was terribly close to a military base that happened to be a prime target for B-52's. The location wasn't by accident and no matter how much the UN Observers wrote up reports claiming it was too damn close, the reports went completely ignored by the local government.

Whoever determined where exactly the hospital should go had a very disturbed sense of humor. The medical facility sat directly in line and at the end of the longest runway on the base. It may have seemed expedient at the time to have a crashing plane end up in front of the emergency room, but anyone who happened to be entering the trauma center would probably be tossed inside by the shock wave.

It was gratuitous for Bishop to be given his own room on the back side of the facility, and away from prying eyes of the gray mice that kept track of everyone coming and going. From his single window he could observe most of the aircraft taking off and was able to identify each plane by the tail section configuration.

He had been a guest of the North's hospice for two days and in that time he was mostly kept unconscious. The blood test conducted shortly after his arrival indicated toxic agents associated with elements from explosives. The original report mentioning liver disease was considered, but ignored due to the fact a Korean doctor had made the prognosis.

This explosive element might not have showed up in the test if it wasn't for Bishop taking a second dose on the flight up. He noticed the effects from the first bit of C-4 were starting to dwindle and to make sure he would be in the appropriate ailment when arriving he took another marble sized piece. This one actually put him over the top.

What was recommended by the North's doctors was plenty of sleep and several bags of intervenes drip to keep his fluids up. The only problem that kept him awake at times was the fluids seemed to puddle in his feet. Each foot was swollen and when he stood it was like standing on a water balloon.

But this was the second day as he lay in his bed starring at the pale blue gym bag with the white globe and locking catch sitting on a small table near the end of his bed. Bishop's package was wrapped in towels and covered with old underwear deep in the bottom of the carrier. And before he and the kitbag were deposited on the Hind helicopter, Alec made sure he was to get 'his' bag back in good condition.

Bishops gaze that included some reflections of the past few days events were suddenly interjected by Major Tennyson's voice asking, "And how is our overly zealous Corporal doing today?"

"Hello Major. Sir" Bishop replied as he wiggled down under the blanket keeping his head out from under.

"They keep this place on the chilly side don't they?"

"It helps to keep the ice cream frozen."

"What ice cream?"

"Figure of speech sir."

"Oh yes, more American colloquialisms eh?"

"Kinda like that sir."

Tennyson moved closer to the Corporal's bed in an attempt to be more congenial, but it only made Bishop feel like he was being attacked.

"So," Tennyson began. "They tell me you can get back to work tomorrow."

"I don't know sir. I'm still feeling a little sick if you know what I mean?"

"Oh come on Corporal. Anyone who eats plastic explosives for breakfast must have an incredible constitution."

Bishop grimaced and pulled the blanket up under his chin.

"I suppose going to the dumper is a bit tricky eh?"

"There's a fire extinguisher by the door sir."

"Then I suspect you have all the comforts of home?"

Bishop rolled over on his side facing Tennyson. He now had the blanket up over his nose.

Tennyson looked around for a chair and spotting one by the door where he came in went over and retrieved it. Dragging it across the floor the steel legs made a heck of a screeching sound, like fingernails across a chock board. He placed the chair beside the bed and sat down. He was less than two feet from Bishop's half exposed face.

"So Warrant Officer Harper tells me you've been very successful in your information gathering."

Bishop realized the conversation had just shifted gears and his attention would be fully employed. It was time to get down to business.

"Yes sir," Bishop replied. "The package I told you about, or at least part of it is over there in my bag."

Tennyson looked at the kitbag on the table and then back to Bishop.

"You say part of it?"

"Yes sir. I grabbed two of the devices. One for use and one for parts."

"So both of them are in there?"

"No sir, I had to give one to some damn dink Captain to buy my ride up here. Sir"

Bishop knew he could say just about anything to an officer as long as he stuck the word 'sir' on the end of it.

"Lucky for you laddie," Tennyson said as he rose and went over to take charge of the bag. Picking up the somewhat heavy carrier he added, "We're not really sure what to do with it. We can't give it to the North, besides you've already done that. And we can't return it to the American's because they had to have given it to us through proper channels, and they haven't."

"I guess the best thing to do is bury it in the basement of the embassy, sir"

"That is an option."

"I was wondering if you heard anything about Captain Benjamin?"

"Who's he?"

"The pilot of the downed plane sir?" Bishop replied wondering why the major was being illusive on the subject.

"We don't get any response from the South once we have turned in our 1024, Belligerent Action Report."

"I see sir," Bishop said as he tossed off his blanket and sat up on the side of his bed.

Tennyson moved to the door, but before opening it he turned back to the Corporal.

"Alec sent me another report yesterday. It seems the Americans decided to drop a hell of a lot of bombs on that downed plane," The Major said casually. "They carpet bombed a path about a half mile wide and at least one mile long."

Bishop began to grin. "More urban renewal sir?"

Tennyson paused and smiled. "Sergeant Wilkins will be over late this afternoon to pick you up. Be ready Corporal."

Bishop slid off his bed to the standing position. He was dressed in an NV Army shirt that covered his underwear. It was the only hospital dress he had received.

"Yes sir."

TO BE CONTINUED!

BOOK TWO

BISHOP'S RESOLUTION

COMING IN FALL OF 2012